Nathanial Thatcher

3

The Diamond Trials

The Diamond Trials

T.C. Chappell

Blue DOT Books

Nathanial Thatcher: The Diamond Trials
Text copyright © 2019 by T. C. Chappell
Book Cover by Neil Chartier
Cover Art © 2019 Blue Dot Books

For information address Blue Dot Books at
BlueDotBooks@Yahoo.com

ISBN-978-0-9983388-3-5

Library of Congress Control Number:2019954310

10 9 8 7 6 5 4 3 2 1

First edition, Nov 2019

"The best way out is always through."

-Robert Frost

CONTENTS

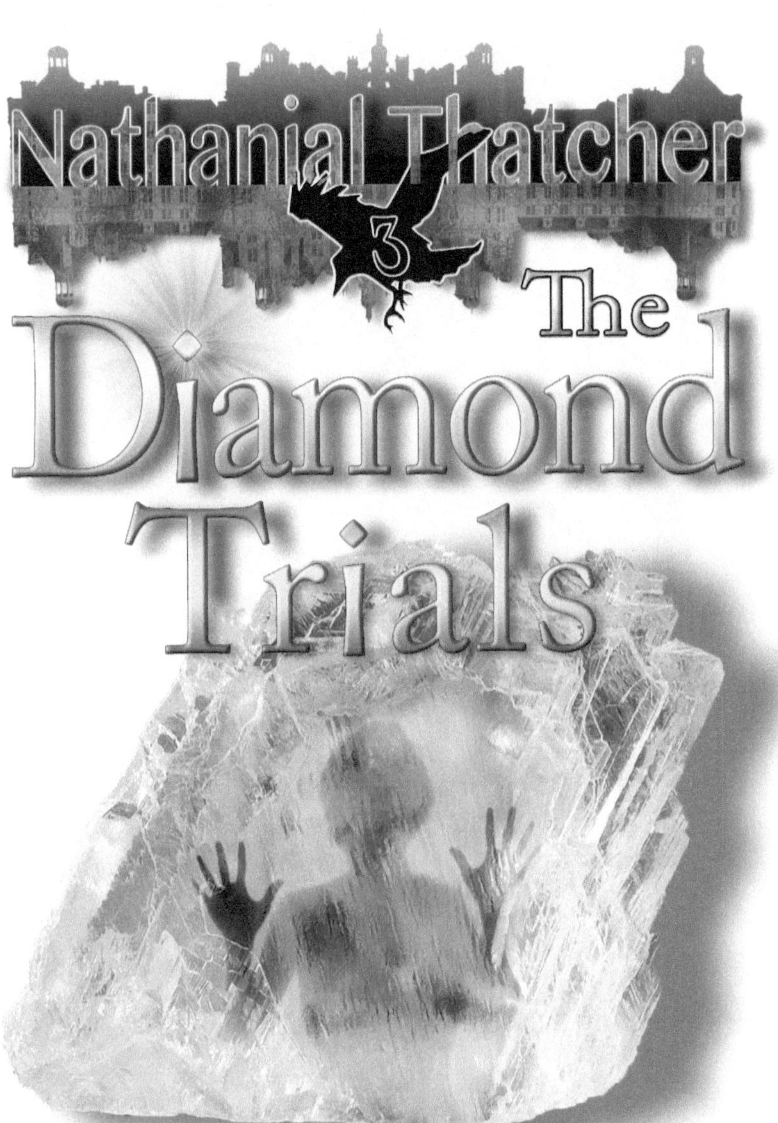

Nathanial Thatcher 3

The Diamond Trials

T.C. Chappell

Chapter 1

A City of Swartza

It was a crystal-clear night, beneath a blanket of stars, and a tiny fire crackled on the spotted branch of a tree in an old aspen grove. A hunched silhouette kept close to its warmth and added a handful of twigs to fuel the flames.

"I can't believe we've been flying for over a week now," the tween-age boy complained, seemingly to himself, as he pushed back his scruffy dirty-blond hair out of his brown eyes and behind his pointed ears. "Boss has probably filed his inquiry and gotten Aliya back by now. Maybe I shouldn't have been so hard on him. This was stupid." He stretched his shoulders from side to side and reached back to scratch an annoying itch deep between his shoulder blades.

From the tree branch above, a black raven fluttered down and landed to tower over the inch-tall sprite boy.

"Did you get 'em?" The boy jumped excitedly.

In response, the raven dropped a mouthful of grubs the size of the boy's arms by the fire. The sprite swished out a knife from a sheath strapped to his calf and sliced up the five wiggling worms until they lay motionless. He threw the bodies onto some thick sticks that were propped over the fire.

"I knew I heard them squirming up there," the boy laughed. "I'm assuming you've already had your fill?"

The raven cawed. The boy took a canister over to a dangling leaf and angled the leaf's green point into the canister's mouth. Water flowed from the leaf and filled the canister to overflowing. The boy took a swig and sat back down by the fire.

Staring into the orange flickers, the boy started to shake his head. He sighed and said, "Yeah, this is weird. It feels like I've been two different people, you know? Like Nathanial Thatcher was some sad, sickly kid from another life and now I'm Nat!" He held his knife in the air and raised his voice, saying, "The sprite! Rider of ravens and eater of grubs!" Nathanial laughed briefly but soon dropped his arm and frowned. He poked one of the cooking grubs. "Who am I kidding? I'm still Nathanial Thatcher. It doesn't matter how pointy my ears get." He lowered his voice to a whisper before admitting, "I miss Mom." He glanced sideways at the raven, who quickly looked away so as not to see Nathanial's oncoming blush.

Nathanial rose and used his knife to pull the grubs off the fire. He cut off some tender pieces, skewered them on the point of his blade, and blew away the heat before scarfing them down hungrily. He did this several more times before rubbing his distended belly.

"Who would have thought bugs could be so tasty?" Nathanial said with a burp. "You want the rest?"

The raven didn't need to be asked twice and he gobbled the leftover bug bits straight off the fire.

"Well," Nathanial said, cleaning off his blade with his jeans and sliding it back into its sheath, "I feel pretty rested. You said we're close, right?"

The raven cawed.

"How do you feel about finishing this trip tonight?" Nathanial asked hopefully.

The raven tilted his head, then clicked his beak.

"Great!" Nathanial said and put his water canister into his rucksack before slinging the pack over his shoulder and springing up onto the raven's neck with a flea-like jump. "You know, you're not bad at all. I bet these Swartza guys just got a bad rap. I mean, why else would you work for them?"

The raven cawed and stomped the little fire out with his talons before taking off into the night air.

It was usually too cold to ride at night, but

Nathanial's determination acted as his shield and the injustice done to his captured friend burned hot within him. Aliya was the most honest person he'd ever met, and after spending time with pressuring peers at his human school and tricky sprites training to steal from humans at his sprite school, this quality had become even more endearing to him than it had been back when he'd first met her over a year ago. She was very far from deserving the treatment she had suffered. A blood curse had been set upon her for some wrong done by a long-dead maternal relative, and that was just beyond unjust. It kept her perpetually in despair. No dream or goal of hers could come to fruition under this curse. Proof of that lay in the six years of her life that had been stolen away by a heartless sprite keeper, Cyron. He'd held her prisoner aboard the pirate ship Argosy, stuck in a loop of time, each day the same as the one before, never aging, never remembering, always reaching for a wish that would never be granted. Aliya wouldn't have even realized she was endlessly repeating her days if Nathanial hadn't pulled her off that ship.

But in the end, the blood curse had reared its poisonous head again. The truth was that the prison ship Argosy was the place that had been keeping her alive, and she would have to return there or let the blood curse run its course through time and send her to an early grave. Nathanial had seen it in her eyes when she was told this, she was not sure which fate was worse, and that knowledge twisted like blades within Nathanial's chest.

Nathanial let the rushing air fill his lungs and cool the fires of anger that had been stoked by the memory. He was now on his way to fulfill the promise he'd made to Aliya, that he'd come for her if ever she were taken back to that ship of nightmares. He'd been delayed by forced memory loss and maneuvered into a deal with the Swartza to free her, but nevertheless he was on his way.

Why did the Swartza want Nathanial to join them? They hated humans and knew he used to be one. The Swartza had offered Aliya's freedom from her keeper on only one condition. He and Aliya were to allow themselves to be taught by the Swartza, to become Swartza; and what little he knew of them was not good. They were an elitist group bent on making sprites the dominant species. They had no empathy for humans or any other creature on the planet. They were basically the worst kind of sprite and exactly the sort Aliya had always warned him about. Was he freeing her from one prison to guide her into another?

Nathanial shook away the darkening thoughts

and tried to stay positive. He told himself to take it one step at a time. The priority was getting to Aliya and stopping the blood curse. If the Swartza wanted them bad enough they would have to cure Aliya, and then she and Nathanial would figure out the rest together.

He pictured their reunion, and nerves crocheted a knot into his bug-filled gut. His mother had mentioned his growth spurts numerous times, and he imagined Aliya realizing how long she'd been stuck on the Argosy just by the look of him. She wouldn't know that he'd lost his memories. Would she be angry with him for taking so long?

Then there was the small matter of expecting Nathanial to be human, and she kind of hated sprites. Maybe he should shrink his ear tips until he explained.

The raven began to decelerate and decrease its altitude. Nathanial peered down around its beak and began to make out a twinkle of lights within the dark mountain valley. It was such a wide spread of lights that Nathanial first mistook it for a human settlement, but the lower they flew the better he saw that the streets, homes, and clumped tower buildings were well below the treetops and nestled down at grass level.

They flew over the spread-out city for at least

another two minutes before they came to an immense castle-like structure on a hill where all the streets ended. Nathanial was thoroughly surprised by its enormity. The only other time he'd seen sprite architecture of this magnitude was when he had found Midtown. The buildings had been carved and molded straight from the rocky mountain face and camouflaged so well that even if a human could see things made by sprites, they would have missed Midtown. This structure, however, was boldly built straight up and out in the open. There was no shame or concealment here. It dared to be seen by any and all who came across it.

The raven swooped around the back of the castle's jagged black towers and landed on a perch built on an oval balcony. It bent its head down toward the dark marble floor and Nathanial jumped down onto the smooth surface. He peered up at the razor-sharp protrusions that lined the outside castle walls, and his gaze stretched onward into the Milky Way of the night sky. If the architect's goals had been awe and intimidation, then they had succeeded.

Nathanial gulped and looked back at the raven he had come to think of as his comrade. The past week had felt more like a month. It had been his first time alone in a wilderness survival situation, but he'd quickly come to realize that he wasn't truly on his own. The raven had not only helped him find food, but often sheltered Nathanial under his wings in inclement weather and somehow even opened up conversations in moments of loneliness or doubt. They did not use language, but the raven's thoughts and emotions were expressed so clearly that Nathanial knew what he was saying.

The raven nudged Nathanial toward the tall open doors at the end of the long balcony. The boy took a few timid steps forward before quickly turning back again.

"Hey," Nathanial said, thinking fast, "if I want to see you again, how will I find you? Would I just call Raven, like I did before, or would that just bring the closest one?"

The raven tilted his head and cawed three times consecutively.

"Oh right," Nathanial laughed, "of course you have a name. Why didn't you tell me it before?"

The raven cawed more quickly and agitatedly, with clicking sounds to boot.

"Okay, Okay, I should have asked," Nathanial said, calming the bird by petting its beak. The raven hushed and closed its eyes. "Huh," Nathanial smiled in surprise, watching the effect of his touch on the bird. "So maybe I'll see you later then...

Sidian."

Nathanial turned away, reached past his nerves to take hold of the strength within him, and marched toward the warm open light that beckoned from within the cold castle.

WHAT DIAMONDS KEEP

Nathanial walked into a cathedral hallway. Crystalline shards reached down from a basalt ceiling to form clustered chandeliers of light. The red marble tile stretched on ahead of him and the walls were gothic volcanic rock. He could hear his own footsteps echo throughout the open space as he continually forced one foot in front of the other.

Voices sounded from an undetermined distance ahead, and Nathanial stopped in his tracks. He was about to have company, and there was nowhere to hide.

Two tall figures entered Nathanial's passageway from an opening just ahead of him. The figures stopped upon seeing him, and the strange silver fastenings on their dark business attire chimed softly before silence fell. The dark green sprite on the left smiled, satisfaction glinting in his black eyes at seeing Nathanial's frozen form.

"Ah, finally, my appointment has arrived," he said to the red-skinned man who reminded

Nathanial creepily of Darth Maul, though no horns sprung from his bald head.

Nathanial swallowed a knot of air down his dry throat. This jade-green Swartza was the one who had first shot at him with an arrow, taken his memories, and attempted to kidnap him before finally offering a truce and the return of Aliya, which Nathanial was now counting on. It was strange to see him out of his creepy cloak. His hunter-green hair was long enough for a ponytail but instead clung like greasy seaweed around the base of his neck. A high collar perfectly matched the tall points of his ears. His usual scowl had been swapped out for a pretentious half smile. Nathanial did not much like the change.

"If you'll excuse me, I must take this one directly to Lady Seizette," the proud figure said with a goodbye bow, ignoring his bald companion's curiosity and approaching Nathanial. "So glad you decided to join us, Nathanial."

A thousand objections ran through Nathanial's mind at the insinuation that he had joined something, but he wanted to get Aliya back and decided to lead with that point. "You said you could get me Aliya. I've come to see if it's true."

"Of course it's true," the Swartza said, gesturing Nathanial forward and walking with him down the hall. "In fact, she is here already. When I saw you were coming I sent for her."

"Really?" Nathanial said, afraid to believe it. "Can I see her now?"

The Swartza moved his head from side to side, saying, "Soon. There is someone you must meet first."

Nathanial followed in silence. They had turned down a claustrophobic hallway where cement sculptures jutted out from the walls in forms of screaming, reaching, half-buried sprites. It was the most unsettling hallway Nathanial had ever had the misfortune to walk through. Why would anyone have a place like this?

So he was pretty surprised when they exited the shadowy hall of silent screams and emerged into a glimmering, immaculate room. Pink silk couches with golden trim encircled a sparkling coffee table with giant flowers that umbrella-ed out of a quartz centerpiece. The carpets were woven with beautiful blue-and-silver geometric swirls. The ceiling was high and made from individual carved maple blocks that interlocked into large quadrangle patterns...and the walls! Nathanial wasn't certain, but it looked as though the large spreading crystals within the otherwise speckled rock were towering diamonds!

The Swartza continued across the room. "Take a seat. It might be a few minutes," he said and exited through a giant oak door.

Nathanial considered the light color of the upholstered cloth against his jeans, now grimy from a week of roughing it, and thought it best not to take the sprite's advice. He was more interested in checking out the walls anyway. He went over to one of the larger diamond veins that stretched from floor to ceiling. Running his hands across its surface he could see the light sparkle like rainbows between his fingertips.

"Beautiful, aren't they," said a sultry voice from the oak doorway.

Nathanial started and turned toward the voice. Not even a minute had passed, plus the woman who stood there was not what he had expected. She was beautiful.

"Diamonds are an amazing crystal," she said, walking toward Nathanial with a natural sway to her movements, her evening gown sparkling and her high heels clacking with every step. "Not only are they stunning to look at but they are strong and intelligent."

"Intelligent?" Nathanial repeated, confused at the implication.

"Yes," she said with a shimmering red-lipstick

smile that contrasted with her ivory skin. "They can hold immense amounts of information. I should know. I help them grow. You could almost say I'm like a mother to them."

That might explain the glimmering skin, Nathanial thought. She was almost hard to look at yet he couldn't take his eyes off of her. Even her long, sleek ebony hair could catch the light and shine like a rainbow; two silky hair strips cascaded into sharp tips in front of her pointed ears, accentuating their diamond-studded beauty. Her form-fitting dress was made entirely of black diamonds except for the hourglass shape of clear diamonds that streamed down from her collarbone to her waistline like a waterfall of wealth.

"My name is Seizette," she said upon reaching him and held out her hand in a peculiar fashion, with her fingers turned down.

"I'm Nathanial," he said. He took her fingers and shook them. Even if he had had an inkling he was supposed to kiss her hand, he was too busy falling into the galaxy he could have sworn was spinning within her eyes.

Seizette breathed her amusement and Nathanial quickly dropped her hand with a blush.

"I'm afraid you've caught me during a business party," Seizette said, still smiling, "but I had to come say hello."

Nathanial lifted up onto his toes and then went back down with a "Hellooo."

Seizette laughed. "Well, I want to give you your little friend back before I return to the party," she said approaching one of the diamond columns on the far back wall. "She has been an amazing wealth of information, a real pleasure to have. I'm excited that you'll both be staying with us."

Seizette put her well-manicured hand on the diamond and closed her eyes. Nathanial took a few steps closer. He couldn't believe what he was seeing. Aliya was forming within the crystal. First he could see her brown, curly hair and soon her splash of freckles over her olive-skinned nose. She was still wearing the knee-length maroon dress with patchwork pants, high brown boots, and a long-sleeved, waist-length black jacket that she'd used to disguise herself as a sprite hoodlum back in Midtown. Once she appeared solid, Seizette reached her hand into the crystal and pulled Aliya out.

Nathanial ran forward, seeing Aliya was weak and about to collapse. He caught her before she hit the floor. Then he looked up at Seizette, not sure what to say.

"She'll recover shortly," Seizette said, still

smiling. "I look forward to talking with you again, Nathanial. We have much to discuss." She turned and headed back toward the oak door. "I'll have Jerald come fetch you two to your quarters."

She was almost through the open door when Nathanial suddenly panicked and shouted, "Wait!" Seizette halted to look at him. "She has a blood curse. She could die," he said desperately.

Seizette smiled softly at his obvious care for Aliya and said, "I left a bit of my diamond within her. It will contain the spreading curse…for now."

Relief and uncertainty churned within Nathanial then he saw two figures looking back at him from the posh business party beyond the door. One was Cyron, his skin underneath his navy suit still the color of the open sea. The other, towering above the rest like a puffed-up toad, was the large sprite from headquarters, the boss of Boss, his green ears as jagged as his soul. He'd once been responsible for keeping Nathanial so sick he'd had to be confined to his sterile bedroom for most of his life.

The door closed behind Seizette, leaving Nathanial numbed by what he'd just seen. His enemies were within these walls and he may have just agreed to a deal with them.

He tried to force his attention back to the goal at hand. He'd crossed the country more than once in the past two weeks, trying to reach Aliya, and he almost couldn't believe she was right here in his arms.

"Aliya? Aliya, can you hear me?"

Aliya groaned. Nathanial tried to get her to her feet. She seemed to be responding. He was able to carry her over to the couch and sit her down. She lifted her head, but her eyes remained closed.

"Aliya?" Nathanial tried again.

"Nathan?" Aliya moaned. Her slight Hebrew accent sent joyous butterflies fluttering though his stomach. It was so good to hear her voice. "Nathan, did it work?"

Nathanial furrowed his brow. "Did what work, Aliya?"

"Your wish!" she responded as if he shouldn't have had to ask.

"Oh." Nathanial's heart fell. It was as he feared. She had no idea how long it'd been since they were at the wish-sprite hearing together. It was probably yesterday to her, if not the same day, even. She thought their plan had succeeded and his wish to change sprite law had been granted. That he was there to take her home because now all sprites would be required to ask humans for permission and pay compensation to work on them, and neither of them would consent to be used that way anymore. How was he going to break the truth to her?

Aliya opened her dark eyes. "Where are we?" she asked, looking at the giant flowers in front of her. "Last thing I remember was being dragged back aboard that horrible ship."

"Um…" Nathanial cleared his throat.

Aliya blinked and turned her head toward him. Her eyes widened, and he braced for impact. "Nathan," she said slowly, "you have pointy ears."

"Yeah." Nathanial licked his lips. "About that…"

A man entered the room through the oak door. He wore a beige tailcoat jacket over a white button-up shirt with a red bow tie. His colors were a little splotchy around the cheekbones but he was mainly yellow, and his straw-like hair was bowl-cut. He stopped in front of Nathanial and Aliya, who both looked at him, dumbfounded.

"I am Jerald. I have been instructed to show you to your quarters," he said rather snootily.

"What's going on?" Aliya asked, with a touch of panic catching in her throat.

"I'll have to explain later," Nathanial said, helping Aliya stand. "We should probably go with him for now."

Nathanial held tight to Aliya as they followed Jerald through the strange passageways of the castle. Occasionally her knees would buckle and he'd have to help her back up.

Finally, after the trio had gone through several corridors where the diamonds shone through the cracks in the volcanic rock walls, they spiraled down two stone stairwells, walked along a hall adorned with fancy paintings of fancy folks wearing fancy clothes, and came to a long hallway lined with tall doors on both sides.

Jerald stopped in front of one of them and reached for the brass doorknob in the center of its iron frame. He pulled it toward himself, until it clicked, then moved the knob along a labyrinth-like path in the door. There was another click, and the door opened.

"This room is for the young lady," he said dryly.

"Oh," Nathanial said, surprised, "you're splitting us up?"

"Girls and boys do not dorm together," Jerald responded flatly.

"Right." Nathanial groaned and helped Aliya into the room.

Inside, the light grew bright automatically, as if sensing their entrance, and the entire ceiling came to life with the glow of its painted flowers. A massive canopy bed sat in the center of the room, with purple flowers twisting along the vines that draped like curtains around it. The entire room had a theme of vines and flowers. Twisting maroon branches formed the bones of chairs, tables, and dresser drawers, while pink silk cushions fluffed with rosy patterns topped any sitting surface. Nathanial took Aliya over to a small couch. She sat and bent her head down into her arms.

"Are you okay?" Nathanial asked, hurting to see her like this.

"Just a headache," Aliya moaned.

"Come with me, please, young sir." Jerald gestured to Nathanial to exit the room.

Nathanial sighed. "Well, maybe it's best you get some sleep before I catch you up on things anyway."

Aliya moaned again in response. Nathanial slowly walked toward the exit. "I'll see you tomorrow, okay?" he said, hating to leave her so soon after he had found her.

The door closed and a mechanical clank sounded. "You're locking her in?" Nathanial asked.

"Everyone is locked in for their own protection," Jerald answered.

Nathanial was greatly relieved when Jerald only took him to the room next door. The sprite decoded the pathway on the door with the knob that was set within the metallic labyrinth-lock. The many left and right turns Jerald made along the crisscrossing paths that covered the entire surface of the door seemed different to those he had used on Aliya's, and Nathanial soon lost any hope of memorizing the code.

His room was thankfully less flowery than Aliya's. The opaque marble ceiling glowed upon entry, and he was glad to find that he had a giant canopy bed of his own. It'd been a while since he'd slept comfortably. The room seemed hard, with the frames of his bed, chairs, and cabinets all black steel, but the red-blanketed mattress looked cushioned enough.

"I expect I will be the one waking you in the morning," Jerald said.

"Oh," Nathanial said. "Okay."

Jerald exited and Nathanial heard the clank of the door locking. He went over to the door to try the handle and check that it was locked, just for good measure, but there wasn't even a knob on this side. He tried pushing the door anyway. It wouldn't budge.

It was time to get the lay of the land. He opened all the drawers and found clothes in them. There were dark blazers with a logo patched onto the breast pocket of silver keys crossing a sword. He had seen the symbol before on a Swartza's ring. It must be their coat of arms, he thought.

Nathanial rushed to the windows and opened the heavy burgundy curtains. He saw a small balcony outside the set of double-windowed doors. Swinging them open, he rushed out onto the landing and checked if Aliya's lights were still on when he felt a sudden wave of faintness. He'd leaned too far over the stone banister. The immense height had caught him off guard. He was high up in one of the castle towers and could see the sparkling lights of the city he had flown over stretching out below him. The vertigo passed, and now, prepared for the height, he leaned back over, ready to call Aliya's name.

Aliya opened her balcony doors before he made a peep.

"Nathan?" she said, presumably hoping it was him in the darkness.

"Hey, yeah, it's me!" he whispered excitedly. "You feeling any better?"

Aliya came the rest of the way out and leaned toward him. "Yeah, I think so." She noticed how high they were. "Whoa." She gulped before recomposing herself. "This place is crazy. I'm locked in. How about you?"

Nathanial nodded. "Yeah, me too. Jerald said it's for our own protection, but I trust him about as far as I can throw him."

"What is this place?"

"Not sure exactly. I know the people here are part of a sprite group called the Swartza."

Aliya's eyebrows just about disappeared into her hairline. "My Mataunte told me about them."

Nathanial couldn't help but smile at this. He missed hearing the stories that Aliya's Mataunte had told her growing up. It was thanks to these stories that Aliya knew so much about sprites.

"They do bad things to get what they want," Aliya added.

"Yeah, but haven't you said that about all sprites in general?"

Aliya thought on it. "I think it's these guys that help to make it all legal."

"Hmm, then you're not going to like this. They want to teach us. I saw uniforms in my drawers. I think there's a school here."

"You're kidding me, right? You aren't thinking about staying here, are you?!" Aliya gaped, unbelieving.

"No," Nathanial said in quick self-defense, but he was thinking of the deal he'd made. Yet he hadn't exactly signed anything or even verbally agreed. He'd just done as much as he had to do to reach Aliya. Would she understand that? Should he tell her or just make a run for it? He felt stuck between a rock and a hard place.

"What?" Aliya asked, seeing the wheels turning behind Nathanial's shifty eyes.

"Nothing," he said quickly and searched for the grace he needed to explain this without completely losing Aliya's confidence in him.

Aliya sighed, "Well, at least I'm off that god-awful ship. Did you have something to do with that?"

Nathanial's heart skipped with delight. "Yes, I knew how much you hated it there and I told you if they took you back I'd just have to come pull you off again. It wasn't easy and it's kind of a long story…"

But before he could take his next breath, a troop of sprites in official-looking uniforms flew down from a walkway overhead. Their high-collared jackets were complete with strings of silver buttons that bore the mark of keys crossing a sword.

"What are you kids doing out of bed?" the biggest sprite of the group asked. A light emitted from his palm, illuminating Nathanial and Aliya.

"These are the newbies we were told about," a second sprite said with a smirk.

"Oh," said the first. "Then we'll let it slide this once, but you two need to learn the rules. There's a curfew and if you break it again you'll be punished."

Nathanial and Aliya looked at one another, horrorstruck.

"Go on, then," the second uniform said, still smiling, "get on back into your rooms."

Nathanial and Aliya did as told. Nathanial shut his curtains and went to lie in bed, but with the new weight of his current predicament on him, a feather mattress was no comfort.

NEW SCHOOL, NEW RULES

Nathanial was busy fleeing a lava flow when the sound of drawers shutting woke him and he sat straight up in bed, gasping. He glared at the man holding a uniform out before him.

"I will only be here for you this one morning," Jerald droned. "I have instructed your bed to wake you at sunrise from now on, and your door will open when it is time for you to go for breakfast. I will show you the way when you are dressed." He laid the clothes down on the bed. "Please shower before putting these on." He pointed to an open door in the corner of the room and shut the velvet curtains of the bed.

Nathanial pulled the uniform toward him and stepped off the bed on the opposite side from where Jerald was standing. He went through the narrow door that had been indicated, and found a shower room that doubled up as a toilet, for the porcelain throne sat directly under a waterfall spout. His experience at Hyperion led him to expect a handprint indentation on the wall, and he found it, but it was smooth rock instead of woody mush.

"All right, then," he said to himself, and hung the uniform on a silver hook next to the door before shutting it. "Let's do this."

After his initial scream as a freezing waterfall crashed down on him, the water warmed up quickly and the shower was nice enough. The soap provided was smoky in smell but not too bad. To his surprise, when the shower hit its auto shut-off phase, a huge gust of wind shot up from tiny holes in the floor. It did a fair job at drying him off.

He quickly put on the white-collared undershirt and black double-breasted jacket with the Swartza coat of arms patched in silver over the breast pocket. It fit smartly, with silver fastenings and trim. Thankfully there was no bow tie for the ensemble; Jerald's ruby-red one had still been blaring from his neck this morning, and Nathanial had worried about being presented with something similar. His khaki pant legs were loose enough to conceal his battle blade, a six-inch-long silver blade in sheath, its gold-and-silver hilt engraved with armor-clad men spiraling up its length. He had become quite attached to the blade and it just felt wrong not to wear it. He hadn't mastered all its potential, he knew, but it had guided him in the right direction, like a compass attuned to his heart, more than once; it'd become a shield that blocked a salamander from making him lunch, and he used it in sword practice with Boss many times.

Nathanial's second most prized possession was the necklace, or more accurately the heavy twisted metal amulet on it, that boosted his ability to tap vibrations and learn sprite tricks. The friend that had given it to him, Mila, had warned him of its illegality, so he kept it hidden under his button-up shirt. It tended to run hot on occasion when he was pushing his limits of sprite ability, but better it give him a red mark on his chest than anyone catch him unable to perform a simple trick and blow his cover. If he had to hide being human born from the open-minded sprites at Hyperion, he didn't even want to think about what this lot might do if they found out what he was.

When Nathanial finally stepped out and around his curtained bed, he was unsurprised to be greeted with a contemptuous sigh from Jerald. Scrutinizing him, the sprite drawled, "Suppose I'll have to do something about that hair," and took a contraption out of a nearby top drawer.

The hair-cutting device was like a handheld vacuum cleaner, with shears buzzing an inch or so inside its nozzle. If the thing didn't look so much like a hungry Cybermat from Doctor Who then maybe Nathanial could have stood to keep his eyes open as it chomped about his head. Thankfully it only took a few head-swirling swipes before Nathanial was given Jerald's permission to pull his nerves together and look into the mirror. His new, shortened, side-swiped hairdo would have appealed to a child brought up on James Dean or Elvis Presley. He, on the other hand, would just have to get used to it. His reflection no longer looked like him. It looked like a kid going to a highfalutin prep school.

Finally, now that Jerald approved, Nathanial was led out of the door and past Aliya's bedroom. He quickly asked, "What about Aliya?"

Jerald kept walking and said, "She's at her appointment."

"What appointment?"

"It doesn't concern you."

"I think it does!" Nathanial said, agitated.

Jerald didn't respond.

When Nathanial stopped glaring sulkily at the ground, he began to notice that the castle didn't feel as foreboding with the early morning light streaming in from the high windows. The volcanic stone walls that had seemed ominously black at night had a way of glistening with blue and gold when the light hit just right.

They turned a corner into a large foyer where loud chatter was echoing from a nearby room. Jerald guided Nathanial into the largest dining hall he'd ever seen. It was overwhelming to see the many hundreds of school-uniformed sprites, ranging from pale thirteen-year-olds to colorful eighteen-year-olds, all sitting along rectangular rows of iron tables, going about their everyday routine in this elongated, gothic-windowed space. This room too had red marble-tiled floors and glistening volcanic walls. He was sure the dozens of quartz-crystal chandeliers that spiked out of the ceiling would glow at night as well.

The strangest part of the scene before him was the way that the students were being served food off silver trays by a hundred or so yellow sprites in beige tailcoats and red bow ties, just like the uniform Jerald wore. It contrasted sharply with the coziness of Hyperion, a school within a towering tree, where kids would serve themselves at mealtimes, choosing from an array of buffet tables that ranged from exotic mystery foods like fire forte to the simple comfort foods of bread and potatoes.

"Your age group sits over there." Jerald pointed to a gathering of about fifty sprites ranged along a table near the closest windows, and then he turned and left.

"Wha…" Nathanial said in shock, watching him go. "Great." He looked back over to his age group table and saw a few eyes looking his way. Here we go again, Nathanial thought, and went over.

"Hey," he said to the group that had been watching him. "Just arrived last night. Guess I'll be taking classes with you guys. My name's Nat." Though this name had been given to him by a sprite he didn't particularly like at Hyperion, and he thought it sounded a little buggy, he also felt like his real name was a little too human and didn't want to chance introducing himself as Nathanial.

The group looked around at each other, surely deciding whether to accept or reject the new kid, until one boy stood up and put out his hand. His hair was swept to the side much like Nathanial's own, like all the boys in the hall in fact, but it was a wavy mix of bright green and ebony black.

"Hello, Nat," the boy said with a perfect smile, "I'm Trid." As Nathanial shook his hand, he noticed a thick ring on Trid's middle finger. Diamonds encrusted the keys and the sword they crossed to form the ever-repeating Swartza symbol. "Have a seat."

A black-and-yellow-streaked-hair girl who was

next to Trid slid down to make room for Nathanial and he took the spot.

"Thanks," he said. He examined the hands of everyone around him but saw no other rings.

"This is Bee." Trid pointed to the girl who had made room for Nathanial. She nodded, her cute bob swishing around honey-colored eyes. "This is Juice." He pointed to the square-jawed youth in front of him, whose thick orange bangs made a perfect croissant-like swirl.

Trid signaled to the closest yellow servant sprite, who hurried over. "Some breakfast for my new friend," Trid instructed the sprite, who promptly turned to the trolley of food behind him and returned to put a plate of food down in front of Nathanial.

"Thank you," Nathanial said to the server. Everyone looked surprised by the gratitude, especially the server, who almost spilled the juice he was pouring for Nathanial.

Trid laughed quietly. "So where are you from, Nat?"

Luckily Nathanial was prepared for this one. Boss had versed him on what to tell the Hyperion students if they asked. "Fayetteville."

"Oh, I see." Trid nodded. "Then you are of the fay sprites?"

Nathanial nodded in return. There was a moment of silence during which Trid looked expectant, so Nathanial asked, "How about you?"

Trid smiled and said, "I'm from here, like most of us, but it's good to have someone from the outside come in once in a while. You must feel privileged."

Nathanial took a big gulp of his juice and kept nodding.

"Wow, two newbies in one day?" the girl across from Nathanial said, peering past him.

Nathanial quickly turned around and saw Aliya standing plastered to the entryway. "Oh, that's my friend; excuse me!" He jumped up and hurried over to her.

Nathanial took a second hard look at Aliya as she stared back at him like a deer in headlights. "Aliya…" He stifled his gasp. "Your ears."

Aliya tried to pull out some loose curls from her finely braided hair in an attempt to cover the new points that so obviously terrified her. She too wore a school uniform, much like his own but tailored for a girl's fit.

"I guess I know how you got yours now." She whimpered, still pushing hair over her ears.

"Uh," Nathanial wondered, "I doubt that. What happened?"

"Some woman said she triggered only what was

within me. She said now that I'm here I needn't worry about the blood curse, but I don't know, Nathan, I don't believe her. Something isn't right about her."

"Seizette?"

Aliya nodded.

"I met her last night. I agree, something isn't right about her." Nathanial suddenly realized that he was in a bad place to be talking about this. More and more eyes were finding their way to the two of them. "We'll talk about it later," he whispered. "Come over here with me and get some breakfast. Just follow my lead to blend in until we can find a way out of here. They like humans as much as you like sprites, so best not to mention it."

Nathanial led Aliya over to Trid's table and introduced them. "Trid, this is Aliya, she's from Fayetteville too. We arrived together."

Trid stood up, took Aliya's hand, and kissed it softly. "How do you do, my lady? Welcome to Swartza High."

Only Aliya and Nathanial seemed to find this gesture odd. Aliya quickly smiled and for some reason awkwardly curtsied. Everyone sat down. The yellow server rushed over and put a plate of food in front of Aliya.

She scrutinized the assortment of chopped

browns, yellows, and reds. Nathanial smirked, wondering if she was recalling the last time she had tried sprite food and almost ate a rat's heart.

"Oh, I bet you don't have these delicacies in Fayetteville," Trid said, watching her expression. "Euthyatira Pudens, Clastoptera, and Fuscicornis." He pointed to each dish as he named them.

"That's a fancy way of saying caterpillar, spittlebug, and fly," the blue-haired girl in front of them said bluntly. "I'm Jozy, by the way."

Nathanial and Aliya smiled at Jozy. She had a kind, round face, sparkles of gray in otherwise green eyes, and blue hair that was tied up with purple beads in a dozen miniature buns, except for two ringlets that curtained her face.

Nathanial settled in to eat his plate of bugs. He forgot how strange that was until he noticed Aliya staring at him. He shrugged and said, "It's good!" He wasn't lying either. He'd been having non-seasoned bug for a week, and this stuff was smothered in butter.

Aliya slowly scooped a slimy red bit onto her spoon and slid it onto her tongue. Nathanial guessed it was an acquired taste because she didn't look to be enjoying it.

A strange humming vibrated through the dining hall and all the kids rose from their tables.

"What was that?" Nathanial said, looking to the ceiling where the sound was coming from.

"It's the school's way of telling us it's time for first class," Jozy said, taking up her satchel and moving along with the group.

"You guys should get here as soon as your door opens tomorrow. There's just enough time to eat," Trid said, standing. "Come on, I'll show you to class."

Nathanial scarfed down the last few bug bites on his plate, while Aliya looked happy enough to be walking away from her hardly touched bits.

They followed Trid down a few corridors and into a stadium-sized classroom. There had to be over a hundred tweens filing in around them. They entered from a doorway at the top corner of the room and made their way down to sit in the middle. It wasn't long before the instructor entered the room from a door at the bottom front corner near a large rectangular desk.

The last couple of times Nathanial had found himself joining a new school, he'd had to introduce himself to the class. He had expected as much again and had his speech all ready to go. His preparation was wasted, however. The teacher did not acknowledge that there were two new faces in the sea. Either he didn't know or he didn't care.

Nathanial found it hard to listen to what the teacher was saying. He was examining the sprites around him, with all their posh uniforms and similar haircuts, all being from rich families and all from the same place. He couldn't help but think, So this is what it would be like if Slytherin had gotten his way, all the pure bloods happily learning together. He laughed to himself.

"You there." The professor was pointing at Nathanial but he didn't notice. Aliya elbowed him and Nathanial looked from her to the professor.

"Um, yes?" Nathanial asked.

"Come down here."

Nathanial checked around to make sure it really was him being addressed. When all the eyes on him confirmed it, Nathanial stood up to scoot his way past all the blocking knees and took the twenty-odd steps two at a time to finally halt in everyone's forward view.

"Why don't you demonstrate what I was just explaining to the class," the professor said.

Nathanial read the professor's nametag. Mr. Hutchince didn't seem to like him very much. He had a concrete-gray tone to his skin, which was appropriate for the stony expression he wore. His salt-and-pepper hair swished over the right side of his head, obscuring one pointy ear.

Nathanial cleared his throat to stall for time. "Demonstrate," he repeated.

"Yes."

"What you were just telling the class?"

Mr. Hutchince nodded.

"Just now?" Nathanial added for a final delay. The class giggled in low tones.

The professor pursed his lips. "Must I reiterate?"

"Yes, please!" Nathanial pointed to the air. "Just so the class can be sure of what it is I am about to demonstrate."

"Mm-hmm," the professor said, stepping back. "The forget trick. A crucial trick every sprite should know in case of emergency when working on or near human factories. If the trick on their sight should fail and they see you, use the forget trick. If you have taken something from the room that they have come to get, use the forget trick. Now, can you demonstrate for the class the forget trick or not?"

Nathanial lifted his eyebrows and couldn't help but say, "Oh sure." He was almost excited, because he had accidently used this trick once before, but then he honestly admitted, "I would, but it seems

I've forgotten how."

The class giggled more openly this time. Mr. Hutchince sneered.

Suddenly Nathanial's vision blurred. The room seemed to brighten and everything blended into a single white slate.

Next thing Nathanial knew, the entire class was getting up and leaving. Aliya came down the steps looking obviously disturbed.

"What just happened?" Nathanial asked and started patting his pockets. He felt like he was forgetting something. Was he supposed to have his cell phone? No, that wasn't right.

"The professor performed the forget trick on you and you just stood there the entire time while he went on with his lecture, where he basically just kept reiterating what idiots humans are, by the way."

Nathanial glanced sideways at Mr. Hutchince, who was exiting the room with a sinister smile on his face.

"That's not cool," Nathanial said uncomfortably.

"No kidding." Aliya rolled her eyes.

"Hey, fay kids," Trid called from the top of the room by an exit. "If you don't want to get punished for tardiness you better hurry it up!"

Nathanial and Aliya started up the stairs.

"This is horrible," Aliya said with a whimper. "I finally get away from Cyron to be surrounded by sprites just like him. What are we going to do?"

Nathanial bit his lip. He felt guilty. It was his actions that had led her there, but he had meant to help her, not make things worse. "Don't worry. I'll get us out of here," he said, determined to fix it.

"How?"

Hesitating at the prospect of running, fearing what it meant to break the deal he'd made with Swartza, but wanting nothing more than to give Aliya some hope for once in her life, he said, "I made friends with a raven. If we can just get outside, I'll call for him."

Aliya nodded, looking hesitantly hopeful, and it solidified Nathanial's decision to seek help outside the Swartza walls. They exited the classroom and followed Trid and his friends at a distance. Aliya did a double take at Nathanial. He was at eye level with her.

"How long was I on the Argosy this time?" she asked, crinkling her brow.

Nathanial licked his lips and let out the words like the final crash of a building wave. "Just over a year."

Aliya gasped. After some time she asked, "You said Seizette didn't turn you, so...did it happen at your hearing, then?"

Nathanial was astonished. He knew Aliya to be inquisitive, but this was verging on mind reading. He felt like he was talking to Mila for a moment, a friend from Hyperion who could do just that. He nodded. "Yeah, humans have no rights to change sprite law. I had to come up with something else."

"So you wished to be a sprite?" Her whisper was becoming strained. "That's a little drastic, don't you think?"

"Well, that horrible sprite jerk Cyron had got his way, dragging you back to the Argosy, and I knew I'd never see you again otherwise. Only a sprite can find the Argosy, remember?"

Aliya hesitated. "So, are you saying," she cocked her head, "you gave up your entire human life so… so you could come and find me?"

Nathanial could suddenly feel the pumping of his heart. She was looking at him funny. His lips parted but only hot air came out. She made his actions sound so serious and selfless and… romantic! At the time he had made the wish it wasn't just about her. It was also about not being stuck in his room forever and not being pushed around by all the sprites anymore. And yeah, he did feel protective of Aliya and maybe it was what was in his mind when he made the wish to be a sprite, but right now he felt very uncomfortable with her looking at him that way.

Nathanial almost ran into Trid and was spared the humiliation of responding to Aliya when a teacher joined the group of students gathered in the hallway.

"Good morning, class," said the Irish accent of a pale, freckled sprite whose dark red eyebrows stretched up into her golden beehive-styled hairdo. She was tall and wore a cherry-colored pencil dress with a feminine suit jacket and a fluffy pink bow tie around her neck. Pinned to her right chest pocket were two things: the silver symbol of the Swartza's keys crossing a sword and a shiny nametag reading Ms. Kimble.

"I asked you all to meet me here today because this is the hands-on portion of the class. The last couple of weeks of shadowing left a few of you worried, but once you start to practice transmogrification, I'm sure everything will begin to click into place." Ms. Kimble opened the large brass doors behind her and led the class into a high-ceilinged rectangular room.

Nathanial stopped breathing momentarily. It felt like he'd stepped into a mad scientist's specimen-jar room; only each jar stretched from floor to ceiling. Where there were not jars there were museum-quality glass displays. Perhaps Dr. Frankenstein had taken up taxidermy and these were his creations.

"Here are some transmogrified combination examples that have been most successful in the bio-modification field," Ms. Kimble said as she led the class past a cat with a wolf's head, a porcupine with a snake's head, and a larger creature with so many different parts it was hard to tell exactly what it might have started out as; now it was scaly, with horns, claws, and canine teeth. All of them were monstrous, standing taller than any horse would to a human, but they weren't as big as they could have been considering that the sprites were only an inch tall. "We use this ability to take what nature has provided us and make it better so it works for our needs."

Aliya tapped Nathanial's shoulder and pointed. He followed her gaze and saw a stuffed Odonata, a creature they had rode the year before that was a dragonfly with a seahorse's head.

"Now, remember: because they are creatures of our making," Ms. Kimble continued, "they do not last long when they stray too far from sprites.

Maybe a few days to a week at best. They need to keep a strong connection to the sprite who combined their vibrations or they will eventually fall apart. Also, each bio-modified creature will have its own regiment of medications you must supplement daily to keep its size in check. You don't want a horse head returning to its natural size when you've put it on a horsefly's body." She laughed.

Aliya put her hand over her mouth in shock while the rest of the class tittered amusedly. Nathanial knew she was picturing the same thing he was. They had let their Odonata go free back into the wild. Now they knew what that meant.

Ms. Kimble came to a halt in the center of the room in front of a towering, dark glass case. She waited for the class to settle in front of her and made sure all eyes were on her before she began talking again. "Had we not perfected transmogrification in the field of bio-modification then we may not have done as well as we did in the battle for our beloved Crossing Treaty. What I'm about to show you now is the very same transmogrified beast our hero, General Grantz, used to trample the troop of rebel reinforcements that ambushed our flanks from the south on Mount Lassen!"

The class vibrated with excitement. Ms. Kimble smiled at the expressions of anticipation and put her hand on the dark glass behind her. The blackness faded away to reveal a beast frozen within a massive, army-tank-sized, rough block of diamond, looming inside a display case. It was up on reptilian hind legs, behind which stretched a muscular, whiplike tail. Its torso and head were those of an angry, hump-shouldered grizzly bear, with fierce knife-length claws. And as if that wasn't daunting enough, it had huge leathery bat wings that spread wide above it, and its mouth was open in a frozen roar.

"Wait a second," a kid in front said, sidestepping to get a better look. "There's someone riding the beast!"

Ms. Kimble smiled and nodded appreciatively. "That's right, Tate. This beast is not stuffed like the rest. He has been preserved by our wise and benevolent leader, Lady Seizette herself, to be awakened if we are ever again in a time of need. And that is the real General Grantz you see on the beast's neck."

Everyone moved to the side to get a better look, and amazed chatter filled the echoing room. Nathanial slowly moved around to see for himself.

General Grantz somehow radiated the same gut-twisting aura as the monster he sat on, even in this frozen form. Completely clad in black armor with the crossed keys and sword stamped into his iron chest and shield, he looked as though he were in the middle of the battle Ms. Kimble had been describing. His helmet obscured his face from the nose up and ended in a jagged spiked crown. His gray mouth was left screaming and his right arm was raised high, axe in hand.

Nathanial looked curiously at the axe for quite some time. There was something familiar about it. He moved in closer and could see there were men carved around the hilt, as if frozen in a battle of their own.

His stomach dropped in realization. The general was holding a battle blade.

TRANSMOGRIFICATION

For the hands-on portion of the class, everyone was ushered out onto the bottom floor of a multileveled greenhouse that could have doubled as a zoological park for all the different sorts of caged animals that were spread throughout the bright place. The parrots, peacocks, and puffins screeched out from their brass bars overhead while the ground floor chittered with marmots, moles, and mice inside silver cages that were tucked among the towering ferns and flowers. All the animals seemed to have been sized down, as nothing was more than a couple of sizes larger than Nathanial when rightly they should have been many times his size.

The students sat at stone picnic tables in groups of six, each with a caterpillar and a worm strapped down to fill the length of each table. Trid had been kind enough to invite Nathanial and Aliya to join his group of friends: Juice, Bee, and Jozy.

Nathanial examined a chart of powders at the end of his table and read the measurements alongside the colored pictures. The blue powder was for shrinking and the red was for growing. Different quantities had different effects.

"This is how they get the parts to match up if they come from different-sized animals," he said to Aliya, who was sitting beside him. "It also explains how that peacock doesn't take up this entire room." He snorted.

"It's monstrous," she whispered.

Trid, who was handing around a box of rubber gloves, said, "All right, troops, let's suit up and be the first ones done here. We'll snatch up that extra credit no problem." He picked up a plastic apron that had been lying on the bench, and put it on over his clothes.

Nathanial and Aliya were last to take a pair of gloves. Then they followed Trid's example by putting on the aprons that lay next to them. Jozy sat across from them and watched the worried faces of the duo as they attempted to pull on the rubbery gloves. They kept getting their fingers stuck between holes.

"Trid." Jozy spoke up once her amusement had faded. "The fay kids didn't go through shadowing. Should you give them a rundown before we start?"

"Right," Trid said, looking like he was always pleased to share how much he knew. "What we are going to do is put this vibrations divider"—he held up a gigantic square blade, like the kind a magician uses when separating the two halves of his assistant— "within the two Oligocheata-class specimens. One of us will guide the vibrations in the blade to switch from the left side to the right side of the back halves of the specimens and let the group know when the blade is about to glow. When this happens it is imperative that those on the left push under and those on the right lift over."

"You should be the vibrations guide," Bee said to Trid, pushing a lock of black-and-yellow hair behind her small pointed ear as a tinge of purple colored her pale cheeks.

Trid nodded. "Agreed. Everyone into their places now."

Trid stood up on top of the table, walked between the specimens until he was at their middles, and positioned the blade just above their centers. Nathanial and Aliya slid down the bench to join Juice; Jozy and Bee set themselves up opposite.

"When I tell you, unstrap the back ends," Trid said, looking to one side of the table for acknowledgment, and then to the other.

With a sudden and decisive motion, Trid pushed the blade through the creatures until there was a distinct sound of metal on stone.

Nathanial flinched back in horror, expecting blood or some sort of worm bit to expel his way, but was astonished to see the flesh holding tight to the metal blade as if glued to it.

"Now," Trid commanded.

Juice and Bee unstrapped the back ends of the writhing creature in front of them. Aliya turned pale, and took off toward the greenhouse exit. Nathanial motioned after her but Juice grabbed his arm, his glinting orange eyes looking foxlike as he said, "Don't even think about it, fay, we need you here. Now help me hold this thing!"

Nathanial looked from the teacher following Aliya out the door back to the insistent faces around him. He took hold of the slippery skin in front of him and immediately felt the creature's panicked heartbeat, like an electroshock to his chest.

"Whoa," Nathanial gasped up at Trid, "it's dying! You're losing control!"

It was obvious Trid did not take failure lightly, and he shook his ringed hand in agitation. "Get up here, Nat. I need assistance with these vibrations, now!"

Nathanial jumped up on the table and placed his hands on the blade's handle. He immediately saw blue and green lights popping in his vision. Then he saw the lights had crudely formed the shapes of the worm and caterpillar; the green lights were all trying to touch other greens but were bouncing off a black barrier, and the same was taking place with the blue lights next to it. The barrier had to be the blade, the green lights were the worm, and the blue lights were the caterpillar. Nathanial concentrated. He made the popping lights stick to the darkness until it began to light up.

"The blade's about to glow," Nathanial said, feeling the control build inside of him.

"Yes, yes," Trid stammered. "Do it now!"

Jozy and Bee lifted the back half of the caterpillar on their side while Trid and Juice pushed the back half of the worm under it until the two back halves had switched places.

"You have the hold; you're clear to swap the vibrations," Trid ordered Nathanial.

Nathanial could see the back half of the blue and green lights swapping themselves out through the barrier. He slowly lifted the blade, allowing the two colors to connect, emitting tiny sparks, until the circuitry became whole again.

"It's working," Trid said, watching the two halves mend together as the blade was removed.

Nathanial could feel the creatures' heartbeats calming down, and all the colors turned to turquoise. He finished pulling the blade out and everything felt normal again. There were now two transmogrified half-worm, half-caterpillar creatures squirming before them.

"Whoa," Nathanial said, looking down at the gawking eyes of the troop. "That was intense."

Everyone but Trid began to praise Nathanial in amazement.

"Fully flippant, Nat, no joke, we are sure to get that extra credit," Juice said, thrilled.

"Yeah, what a rush. Nicely honed, Nat!" Bee nodded excitedly.

"I don't think anyone's ever had a successful transmogrification their first time!" Jozy said, flabbergasted.

That remark surprised Nathanial. He looked around and saw dozens of dead worms and caterpillars on the other students' tables.

Nathanial absentmindedly rubbed his chest where his necklace warmed anytime he tried a new sprite trick. "Ugh, that's horrible," he groaned, watching dead worm parts drip gunge off tables.

"Just shows what a good team can accomplish," Trid said, pulling off his gloves. "And we weren't even a full six."

Nathanial could see where he was going with this. The teacher was ushering Aliya back into the room.

"You better talk to her about that weak stomach, Nat," Trid said, leaning in. "We can't have a liability on our hands."

Ms. Kimble stopped in front of their table, her hand on Aliya's shoulder. She took notice of the lively creatures right away. "Wow," she said, beaming, "who was the team captain here? Was it you, Trid?"

Trid smiled confidently and said, "Yes, Ms. Kimble, but I took it upon myself to give our newcomer, Nat, the pleasure of partaking in the vibrations exchange, just to make sure his absence of shadowing would not put him behind the rest of us."

"That was very responsible of you, Trid, and, Nat, I have to say, well done. Well done to all of you." She looked at everyone who was standing around the table. "And without a sixth at that." She glared disappointedly down at Aliya.

Aliya kept her eyes on the ground and her lips pursed. Her skin was no longer pale but hot-poker red.

Nathanial felt horrible. Would she be mad that he hadn't gone after her? He should have. Why hadn't he? Who cared if he angered these sprites in the process? His reason for being there was to get Aliya, and get out, but instead he was learning another sprite trick. It was time to be vigilant: he needed to find a way out of there. Enough assimilating, enough learning with the sprites and about their tricks, even if a part of him was curious and thrilled with each success, he couldn't lose focus. He was too used to playing the secret game, having to hide his human origins from the sprites at Hyperion, and he had fallen right back into that routine. His sprite mentors had trained him well in the art of disguise and he knew that to win his own game he'd sometimes have to play theirs. He just sometimes forgot he was playing a game at all.

"Now, Aliya," Ms. Kimble said, bending down toward her, "can I trust that you'll try harder next time?"

"I'm not a butcher," Aliya said, shooting dagger eyes into the teacher.

Nathanial feared for Aliya then. Ms. Kimble's eyes flickered much the same way a certain fire sprite's eyes had before she'd exploded into a ball of flames.

"I'll make sure she tries harder," Nathanial said, pulling Aliya's arm. "She just needs to remember why we're here. To become stronger sprites."

Ms. Kimble looked pleased with Nathanial's words, at the same time as Aliya looked shocked.

"Very good," Ms. Kimble said, straightening up as the fire died from her eyes. "You all receive extra credit, and for bonus reward you may take a recess before your next class."

The group jittered with excitement and rose to their feet.

"Come on, Nat," Juice said, "you'll love the play yard!"

Nathanial looked pleadingly at Aliya, willing her to just bear with him. She bit her lip apprehensively and they followed the others out of the greenhouse.

The play yard was nothing like Nathanial had expected. First of all, it was in a square courtyard with fifty stories of black stone dormitories towering above them, and secondly, the ground was laid with AstroTurf! Why sprites would ever want fake grass when they could instantaneously grow the real thing wherever they liked, he didn't know. Then there was the matter of the sort of games that were set out for them to play.

Trid picked up a sword from a wall of weapons, flipped it by the hilt, and then pointed it at Nathanial. "How versed are you in war games? Want to show me what you can do?"

Nathanial lifted his eyebrows. He'd had enough sword lessons with Boss to feel somewhat confident in his abilities, but he was sure Trid had trained since birth.

"Ugh, I don't think so. Not today, anyway. That vibration swap really tired me out," Nathanial said, stretching his arms high above his head.

Juice came over with a couple of swords held vertically, and pushed one into Nathanial's chest. "Come on, fay, it's our next class anyway. Show us what you got. Maybe we can give you some pointers." Then he held up his own sword and winked.

"Our next class is sword fighting?" Nathanial asked in a monotone.

Bee picked up three bows, then handed one to Jozy and one to Aliya. "Not just swords," Bee said. "All sorts of weapons. The fourth rebellion could begin any day. We have to learn how to fight!"

Trid came at Nathanial with a sudden swing and Nathanial blocked the blow with a clang. "Wait just a second!" he protested. "Why are we spending our special recess doing exactly what our next class is?"

Juice came from behind and Nathanial had to spin around to meet the attack. "Because it's fun!" he said.

"It's not very fair to have two on one!" Nathanial defended himself from another swing by Trid.

"The rebels don't play fair," Trid said seriously.

Jozy stepped forward with metallic knuckles slipped over her right hand. "At least let him have a pop shield," she said. With a thrust of her fist the knuckles popped out into a shield. She handed it to Nathanial and stepped away.

For a few astonishing moments, Nathanial was able to block each attack as it came at him from both sides. Then Trid changed his tactics, bent low and kicked Nathanial in the back of the knee. Nathanial fell and had two swords at his neck in an instant. He stayed still so the points wouldn't pierce his flesh, but he glared unwaveringly up at Trid.

"Back off!" Aliya screamed at the boys.

"Relax, Mrs. Queasy," Trid said, pulling his blade away, "It's just a game."

"Stupid game," Aliya said, walking over to Nathanial as he got to his feet. "Come on, let's go get some fresh air before class." She turned to Bee and asked, "How do you get out of this place? I can barely breathe in here."

Bee snorted. "You can't leave the building during the semester. It's a lockdown school, didn't you know?"

Aliya turned to Nathanial like her king had just been cornered at chess. Nathanial took a quick breath and said, "Of course we knew, but we didn't think that meant there weren't outside yards for the students to relax in. That's a part of our nature, after all. It's when we are close to the trees and the grass or fresh rivers and the open air that we feel at our best, wouldn't you agree?" Nathanial was recalling this from a lesson he'd had with a nectar sprite at Hyperion, and his week with Sidian had made him feel it was true.

"Perhaps," Trid said, walking toward Nathanial, "and perhaps that's exactly why we must deprive ourselves of that which we crave. We train ourselves not to rely on anything but the strength that is within ourselves. We conquer our own nature first, then nature itself. What can we not accomplish then?" He stopped just a foot in front of Nathanial, daring a rebuttal from him.

"You're right of course." Nathanial pandered to him. "We knew this school was the best for some reason. That's why we came here, to find out."

"Now let's just see if you can handle it," Trid said, smiling, and turned away. "Sprites try to drop out every year, but that only makes it harder on them. You don't want to be sent to Lady Seizette for reconditioning."

"Oh, Trid, that's enough," Jozy cut in. "Nat is awesome. He won't be sent for reconditioning. Look what he did in bio-modification. Look how he took the two of you on just now."

"I'm not worried about Nat!" Trid pointed his sword at Jozy with an intense expression, then looked directly at Aliya.

The walls of the school vibrated, signaling the rotation of classes. Everyone moved to put their weapons back into place and it wasn't long before more students were filing into the play yard. Aliya continued to glare at Trid until Nathanial felt forced to shake her out of it.

"Stop, Aliya," he whispered to her worriedly. "You'll draw attention to yourself. We don't want to make enemies here."

"They are already our enemies, Nathan," Aliya said in his ear. "All sprites are. How do you plan to get us out of here now that we aren't allowed outside?"

Nathanial tried to think. "There was a balcony when I came in. We might have a chance there. Maybe the patrols stay close to the student dorms rather than going up there near Seizette."

"Let's go, then!" Aliya pleaded.

"Now?" Nathanial worried.

"Yes, while classes are crossing in the halls. It's

the perfect cover."

Nathanial scanned the courtyard in a panic to see if anyone was watching them. The situation did have a now-or-never vibe. Trid was meeting up with more friends over by the shields and plenty of bodies were blocking his line of sight if he happened to glance back their way.

"Okay, let's go," Nathanial said and forced himself to take action.

They squeezed out of the door and dodged the incoming students. It was difficult to find his bearings but Nathanial had discovered, in his week of travel with Sidian, that he had a great sense of direction.

"I think it's this way," Nathanial said, peeking out of a window to see where the sun was in the sky, and led them down a corridor.

They went up a spiral staircase and through a large green room before they came out into a volcanic rock hallway with red marble-tiled floors.

"Yes, this is it," Nathanial said, recognizing the hall.

They started running toward the gleaming glass doors, exhilaration increasing their haste, when all of a sudden, a giant shadow obscured the sunshine beyond. There was an awful electric buzzing that resonated eerily within the hall and halted the duo in their tracks.

"Nathanial and Aliya," a snide, amused voice echoed from behind them. They spun around. "Whatever could have brought you two all the way up here during class hours?" It was the horrible tracker sprite, who Nathanial felt was taking the lead as his nemesis over Cyron.

Nathanial glared and wondered if the consequences of breaking the deal he had made with this foe were soon to be revealed.

"Aliya," the Swartza said, stepping forward, "we haven't officially met. Please, call me Captain Malik. It was a pleasure to barter for your release and I am pleased we now have you safely in our care. The wealth of knowledge you brought to Lady Seizette has been a worthwhile bonus. I took a peek at it myself." He smiled and looked to Nathanial. "And to think it was all made possible by our friend Nathanial here. You must be very grateful to him."

Aliya looked uncertainly over to Nathanial. "What is he saying, Nathan?"

"Don't listen to him, Aliya." Nathanial defended himself. "He's just trying to turn you against me."

"Am I?" Captain Malik lifted an eyebrow. "Have I said an untruth?"

"I was just trying to free Aliya from the Argosy.

How was I to know this was just another prison?"

"Then you do admit we made an agreement? I release her from her contract with Cyron and the two of you study at the best sprite school in the world."

Nathanial huffed. "I never exactly agreed to…"

"You came here, didn't you? On the wings of a raven by your own free will, asking to see Aliya? Is that not agreeing to our terms?"

"Nathan, is this true?" Aliya stepped away. "You know better than to make deals with sprites. You have first-hand experience of being a sprite factory. It ruined your life, and the second you break from that contract you walk willingly into another?"

"I—I didn't think of it like that," Nathanial stammered. "But I'm telling you I didn't sign anything, and hey, we are sprites now, we have rights!" He had decided to put his foot down. After all, taking control of his own life was one of the big motivators for him wishing to become a sprite.

"You're right, of course, Nathanial. Sprites do have the right to negotiate their own contracts, and that's exactly what we did on the train. You'll find many sprites are still true to the ways of old, and a verbal contract is as binding as a written one. I told you to call a raven if you agreed to my terms and that's exactly what you did." Captain Malik smiled and began ushering them back down the hall. "I should also mention that Sidian is a Swartza raven. He will only serve those who have taken the diamond oath, and you aren't the type to go for that."

For the first time since cutting the paint off his bedroom windows and opening up to the possibilities of the world, Nathanial felt utterly shut in.

HEDGEBALL

Captain Malik guided Nathanial and Aliya back to weapons training. Nathanial had to join the boys with swords and shields on one side while Aliya had to practice archery on the other. He kept looking over to her but not once did he catch her looking back. She was definitely mad at him.

At lunch, Aliya sat a few places down from the spot she'd occupied earlier. She seemed to be getting close to Jozy. Nathanial even caught her giggling at something Jozy had said, which in Nathanial's opinion was a little hypocritical for someone who called all sprites her enemy.

Nathanial was so bummed; he had been poking at what could have been the leftovers from bio-modification class for so long that Trid finally addressed the issue.

"Look," Trid said confidently, "girls are trouble. There's no pleasing them so stop trying. In fact, they like it better when you don't try. Just play stone and she'll be the one to break first."

"I don't know what you're talking about," Nathanial mumbled. He shoved a morsel into his mouth and chewed slowly.

"Right." Trid snorted. "The next class will get your mind off it anyway, because if you don't focus on the task at hand, you just might lose one, a hand that is." And he chuckled at his own joke.

Nathanial prematurely gulped and had to swig a whole cup of juice to keep from regurgitating his mouthful.

Whatever their next class was, the students had to change into some funky-looking outfits to take part in it. Nathanial had followed the boys into a separate changing room from the girls and was given something that he thought was a quilled throw blanket. On closer examination he found it was a cape, plus armbands, kneepads, and a helmet, all with brown plastic-textured spikes threaded throughout. He came out of the dressing room feeling like he was going trick-or-treating as a porcupine.

All the little spiny students gathered in the middle of an AstroTurf arena. It was like the play yard enclosure, with towering gothic-style levels rising up to an open sky, but a hundred times larger. There were horseshoe-shaped arches made of twisted wood spread throughout the arena, like larger-than-life croquet wickets, and two inclined U-turn ramps, one at each end of the soccer field–sized space, both with three levels of arches within them.

A muscular, orange adult sprite, with pads strapped around him from heel to head, looked at his spread-out class of fifty. No one wanted to get too close to anyone else in their current sharp attire. Stamped on the sprite's pumped-out chest pad, Nathanial saw the name Ref Wrecklet.

"Okay," the ref started, his hands on his hips. "Things got a little out of control last week. I appreciate the gall some of you have but until all of you have that tenacity I'm asking the strong ones to let up a bit. You know who you are." Trid was one of the kids who received the proud yet scornful eye from Ref Wrecklet as he scanned the group. "I heard we have a couple of newbies here. I want them split up so that no one team takes too bad a hit. I'll leave it to the team captains to explain the rules." He put two fingers in his mouth and whistled.

From a dozen holes all around the arena, fifty spikey hedgehogs the size of young elephants scurried into view. They lined up and waited further instruction.

"Oh boy." Nathanial gulped, noticing the

saddles behind their heads.

Trid laughed, saying, "It's okay, buddy. You're on my team. I'll show you the ropes."

The class lined up and each team took a turn calling over a hedgehog. How any of them could tell a difference between the creatures, Nathanial wasn't sure. Maybe because some had white hair around their noses and others had black? When it was time to choose, Trid chose a hedgehog for him, and then began to explain the rules.

"This is a game of colors," Trid said, handing the reins of one hedgehog to Nathanial while holding tight to the reins of his own. "Whatever color dominates the field when the last arch is turned, or when time runs out, wins the game. Easy enough, right?"

Ref Wrecklet approached Trid and handed him a green satin bag. "Your team is green today, Trid. Tate's will be yellow." He looked over to Nathanial. "You ever play hedgeball before, new kid?"

"My name's Nat, and no, I haven't."

The ref shook his head. "Didn't think so. More and more schools are banning it. Such a shame." He headed toward the second convening team with two yellow bags still in hand. Nathanial looked past him at Aliya, who still wasn't looking back at him. She seemed nervous, but Jozy was talking her through everything.

Nathanial sighed and turned back to Trid, who said, "Okay, so we have to turn these arches green."

Nathanial put a hand on the twisted root structure next to him. "How do we do that?"

"Run your hedgehog through an arch when you are in possession of the seed-ball. The arch will flower the color of your team." Trid put his hand in the bag, pulled out a pile of green dust and blew it over his hedgehog's quills. The animal shook and its entire coat turned green. Trid brushed the powder residue off his hand and onto his spikey cape. It too turned green. He handed the bag to Nathanial.

"Run through the arches with the ball to turn them green," Nathanial repeated, and blew the green pile of dust toward his hedgehog, which suddenly sneezed. The dust instantly rebounded back into Nathanial's face, abruptly giving him the appearance of a clump of moss.

Trid doubled over in laughter. "Oh man," he said, trying to catch his breath for several moments. "My ribs hurt."

"Great," Nathanial said, stretching, and tried to pop his aching spine. The area between his shoulder blades felt worse in times of stress, and there were a lot of those lately.

"Sorry, Nat," Trid said, getting hold of himself. "That was the best laugh I've had in a while!" Trid took the bag away from Nathanial, turned his hedgehog green for him, and then handed the bag to another teammate.

Juice came over with his green cape and hedgehog, holding a second green bag and wearing a huge smile. He handed over the bag to another student and said to Nathanial, "Went a little overboard with the powder there, Nat." Nathanial nodded, sarcastically appreciative. "Did you fill our fay friend in on all the tricks, Trid?"

"Why don't you tell him about the ramps?" Trid said, rubbing his ribs. "I need to breathe for a second."

"Sure." Juice perked up. "See the three U-turn ramps on each side of the court? The topmost outer arch gives you the fastest boost, with the best air shoot at the base, but it's hardest to control your exit. The speed is progressively lower as you go down, but you line up better with certain targets. We usually start out aiming for the top to get through as many outside arches in the first quarter as possible." Juice switched to a whisper. "It frazzles the other team."

Ref Wrecklet whistled again, calling everyone to attention. "Mount up! If you don't know how to play the game now, you will soon enough!"

The kids, including Nathanial, flea-jumped onto their individual hedgehog steeds. Nathanial had only recently gotten the hang of this jumping technique himself and couldn't help once again looking over to Aliya to check on how she'd manage. She was the last one on the ground and she was biting her lip. He wanted so badly to go to her and tell her how it was done. With a sudden determined expression, Aliya made the jump. She almost overshot it but grabbed hold of the reins and pulled herself back into place. Nathanial smiled. She'd done a bit better than he had his first time.

"Hey," Trid snapped beside Nathanial. "I need your head in the game. Pick up the seed-stick."

"What?" Nathanial shook off his distraction and saw there was a long white stick, with a netted cup at the end, hooked to the saddle in front of him. He pulled it from the hooks and looked back to Trid for further instruction.

"Now, just hope the seed-ball doesn't come to you for the first quarter, and watch me closely!" Trid instructed.

Twenty-five greens spread out on the left side of the court and twenty-five yellows took formation on the right. The ref stood in the center, making a strange humming sound and holding what looked like a ball of twine. A bee, the size of the ref himself, flew down from the arena's skylight. The ref threw the ball into the air; the bee swooped it up into its six legs and shook some yellow pollen off its rump and into the ball while the chaos of greens and yellows clashed like spikey bumper cars beneath the bee until it finally dropped the prize.

It was Tate who first caught the seed-ball in the net of his stick and ran straight for a wooden arch. The seed-ball released a puff of yellow haze as Tate passed through. Enormous yellow flowers blossomed along the twisted branches. A moment later, three greens converged on Tate and seed-sticks became battering-sticks as they all clanked down upon the seed-ball.

The seed-ball fell free of Tate's net and Trid was right behind him to swoop it up off the ground and into his own net. He ran determinedly toward an outer ramp. Once at the base, he kicked his heels into the hedgehog, ordering it to dive. Nathanial ogled as he watched Trid tuck himself into the saddle, disappearing into the hedgehog's back, and the two became one rolling ball that shot up, around, and back down out of the U-turn ramp, totally Sonic the Hedgehog style. Trid rolled through three arches, causing green blossoms before his hedgehog popped back out into a gallop.

It was all very amusing from where Nathanial was trotting along at a safe distance; hedgehogs bumping into each other, arches exploding into flowers. He was even smiling when the horde started his way, but the closer they came, the more menacing the swinging seed-sticks appeared, and then there was the sudden horrifying realization that the hedgehogs were shooting out spearing quills when they were under attack!

Trid had passed the seed-ball to Juice and Juice had just run through another arch, but he had about ten yellows coming down on him. As if in slow motion, Nathanial realized he was Juice's only opening and Juice had locked eyes with him.

"Nat, catch!" Juice yelled, flinging his seed-stick above half a dozen others. It sent the ball on a direct course to Nathanial.

Nathanial's heart stopped but he automatically raised his seed-stick. He caught the seed-ball and sat there in shock, watching the horde of yellows converging on him. At that moment, Nathanial's hedgehog decided to take charge and started backing up. They went right through an arch and the seed-ball exploded, puffing pollen into Nathanial's face. He sneezed as the green flowers popped open around him. The stress was too much for his hedgehog and it flipped out, tripping over itself, trying to run out of the arch but only crashing into it. Before he could make another move, Nathanial was surrounded by yellow and being battered with seed-sticks. The hedgehog shook violently and sent quills in every direction. Two yellows fell from their mounts and the rest of them backed off. The ref whistled and ran up to check on the fallen yellows.

"What have I told you about pushing your capes back?" Ref Wrecklet scolded the two fallen boys. One had a quill in his shoulder; the other had a gash above his elbow. "Keep your cape closed and you won't get quilled!" The ref stood up and sighed. "Well, looks like these two ruined it for the rest of you. That's a demerit for each of you. Now, get up and I'll take you to the medic. Everyone else go get changed and I'll see you tomorrow."

A few of the kids groaned as they dismounted their hedgehogs. Nathanial sat fuming in disbelief at the way the ref was acting. Getting in trouble for hurting yourself! It was ridiculous.

Ref Wrecklet looked up at Nathanial, who was so annoyed he hadn't noticed he was the only one who hadn't left for the changing rooms.

"Can I help you with something, new kid?" The ref asked coldly.

Nathanial narrowed his eyes and shook his

head before dismounting and moving toward the changing rooms. He caught Aliya standing halfway toward the girls' changing room, looking back at him. They held each other's gaze. It was like she was hoping he was going to say something to the ref. Something about how wrong he had been, how wrong the whole thing was, but he hadn't, and she was disappointed once again. Aliya turned away and joined up with Jozy at the girls' room. It was the last time he saw her that day, and it killed him inside.

WHISPERS IN THE WALLS

Nathanial walked damp-headed down the dormitory hall with a green-stained towel around his neck. He'd already said good night to Trid after refusing to join him for dinner. He just didn't feel hungry, or maybe it was that he'd overheard Jozy saying Aliya had already left for bed. Either way he was done hanging around a bunch of strangers for the night.

Finding himself stopped by Aliya's door, Nathanial stared at the labyrinth around the doorknob. He thought about knocking. Would that even work, or was she locked in for the night? She probably wouldn't answer anyway. Or if she did, with a "Who is it?" he would be unable to respond, in fear that she'd turn him away. These thoughts were futile, and in any case they were interrupted by a distant, ghostly voice.

"Nathanial." The soft feminine voice echoed through the empty corridor.

Nathanial quickly turned first one way then the other, calling out, "Who's there?" but there was no one.

"Nathanial." The voice grew nearer until it was close to his right ear. "Help me."

Shivers ran down Nathanial's spine and panic gripped his throat. He stuttered, "Who—who ar-are you? How can I help?"

"Nathanial, please," the voice called again, but it was fading away. "Find me."

Nathanial swallowed hard. "Hello?" There was no response. "Are you still there?" Nothing. "How can I find you? Hello?" He stood there for a few more uneasy moments then went slowly to his room, his ears buzzing as he strained to hear anything in the silence. The door opened at his touch and he went inside for another restless night.

The next morning, Nathanial was awoken by the posts of his canopy bed grabbing him up under the arms and placing him on his feet at the foot of the mattress. He only screamed a little. It'd become normal for weird things to happen and he was starting to take it in stride. He made a mental note to ask Trid if there was a way to change the setting on his bed to less abrupt.

Once Nathanial finished pulling his shoelaces tight, the door opened of its own accord. Must be time for breakfast. He poked his head out at the students filing through the hall and caught Trid's eye.

"So this is where they put you," Trid said, coming over and looking into his room. "Nice. Every room's a little different. You'll have to come see mine after classes. Come on, it's Tuesday. The best breakfast is on Tuesday."

Nathanial glanced into Aliya's room as they passed by. The door was open and the room was empty. He wanted to tell her about the voice he'd heard the night before. She knew so many random details about sprites; maybe she knew something about this. He'd need to ask for her forgiveness first, and an idea had come to him late in the night as to how he might go about it.

He'd remembered an article from one of his mom's advice magazines, about how women could use positive feedback to encourage preferred male behaviors. It commented on how the male ego often makes it difficult for men to apologize, so if they do manage it, then you should never dismiss it or it may not happen again.

As he and Trid entered the cafeteria, Nathanial was determined to apologize to Aliya with the hope that she knew about this positive feedback idea. He saw her sitting down next to Jozy and went directly over to her.

"Aliya, can I talk to you for a second?" Nathanial

asked bravely.

Aliya didn't look at him right away. She seemed to be having a telepathic moment with Jozy. Jozy lifted her eyebrows at Aliya, who sighed before turning to Nathanial.

"What is it, Nat?" Aliya asked without expression.

Nathanial didn't like Aliya calling him Nat. It felt gross. He thought that was probably why she did it and he began to falter but remembered the article and steeled himself to proceed.

"I'm sorry," he said straight out.

Aliya widened her eyes. "I'll be right back," she said to Jozy and got up from the table.

Nathanial was hopeful as he followed Aliya out of the hall and into a quiet corner. She turned to him seriously and said, "Go on."

"Huh?" Nathanial was confused. He hadn't planned more than I'm sorry.

"What are you sorry for?"

He licked his lips and went with: "Everything."

"Everything?" She didn't seem to be buying it.

"Yes, everything." Feeling his face heat up and the pressure rising, he took a deep breath and just went for it. "I'm sorry for making a deal with these guys that not only put me in danger but put you in danger too. I'm sorry you were on that ship for another year because I lost my memories, which I haven't even had time to explain about, but it was a part of these same sprites trying to revert me back to a factory, and now I have us right in the middle of them. I'm sorry I made a stupid wish to be a stupid sprite thinking it was the only way to take control of the situation since only sprites can change sprite law and only a sprite could find the Argosy, so it seemed to make sense at the time but there had to be another way, which I'm sure you would have thought of but I'm not as clever as you. I'm sorry we're trapped here now with these power-hungry freaks who want to brainwash us and make us into their minions and take over the world and enslave all the humans, which was exactly what we were trying to stop to begin with!"

Nathanial swallowed, his stick-dry tongue dying limply in his mouth, and watched as Aliya's stern expression finally softened into a smile. "Yeah, well, as long as you know it was the whole becoming-a-minion thing that was really bothering me, I guess I can forgive you."

"I really am sorry," he said, relieved.

Aliya nodded and said softly, "I don't mean to be so angry with you. I'm not even sure it is you that I am angry with, more our situation, and perhaps I was blaming you for that, but I'm not sure I could have done any better in your place. You got me off that ship and for that I am grateful." She leaned in and hugged Nathanial. "Thank you," she said, heartfelt.

It was like all the weight was lifted from his shoulders and he wanted to rest there in her embrace forever. When they pulled apart he was recharged and ready to form a plan. "So, how are we going to get out of this mess that I've made?" he asked.

Aliya sucked on the inside of her cheek. "Not everyone here is as evil as I first thought," she said, leaving Nathanial surprised that the sprite-hating Aliya would say such a thing, but he was done talking for a minute. "Jozy doesn't like this school, and she says there are others too, but no one speaks openly about it. They are afraid to not conform and they don't know who to trust. She says she wants to help us and knows a few outside balconies that are less guarded. With her help we could try again."

"But remember what that Malik jerk said? My raven will only follow orders from those who have taken some sort of oath. I don't think he'll come to me."

"I asked Jozy about that. It's the diamond oath, which is taken after the Diamond Trials. A student can go through the trials when they feel they are fully worthy and ready to devote themselves to the Swartza cause. It gives you access to all sorts of resources, like VIP access, but it's supposed to be really difficult. Most wait until their last year to try the trials, but it's not unheard of for those in our year to do it. Trid has done it, so it can't be that difficult, right?"

"Should we ask for his help? Do you think he's like Jozy?"

"Not likely. But maybe you can get him to tell you what the trials are all about."

"And what, take the oath myself? Aliya, weren't you just mad at me for getting suckered into a sprite contract? Isn't this the same thing?" He felt like Aliya was doing a one-eighty here and it had a dizzying effect.

She pondered him with a slightly guilty expression. "I know, but like I said, I'm not sure I could have done better in your place and maybe you were right. Maybe becoming a sprite was the only way to take control of the situation; I mean, we aren't factories anymore, right? And after talking to Jozy about it, I think if you could pass the trials, you would have more rights than even a common sprite. They would have to respect your wishes. You could call that raven and we could get out of here."

Nathanial was gobsmacked. She definitely had done a somersault and was pitching ideas that sounded a lot like ones he would have been scolded for, but she did have inside information from Jozy and maybe it was their best chance of freedom. "Okay," he said, shaking his head. "I've already bound myself up in one horrible contract; maybe another one can counter it. But that means I'm going to have to schmooze, you know, really make Trid think I'm his friend, so it wouldn't hurt for you to lighten up on giving him the evil glares."

Aliya blew a raspberry in exasperation. "I hate pretending."

"I know, me too, but unfortunately it's all these people know how to do and I've had to get good at it to hide who I am. You'll need to try as well. They can't ever know that either of us were human."

"I'll try."

"Then it's a plan!" Nathanial said, excited to have a goal again, or was it to have Aliya smiling back at him? It was probably both.

They sat back down between Trid and Jozy, with Bee and Juice across from them. Trid had been right. The breakfast was scrumptious. Even Aliya enjoyed it. There was sugar toast, pancakes, pastries, and pies. The entire meal had a bread theme with plenty of different-flavored jams and nectars to slather over it. Nathanial was delighted to wash it down with honeysuckle juice, though the reminder of Hyperion gave him a pang.

He was surprised at how much he seemed to miss that school. He supposed the sharp contrast between Swartza High and its strict rules on conforming behavior versus the encouragement Hyperion gave the students to find their own callings from within had something to do with it. He was thinking about all the class choices they had there and really wishing he could have explored the options more.

"So, what classes do we have today?" Nathanial asked, assuming it'd be a different rotation like it had been at Hyperion.

"What?" Trid asked, with an air of amazement at how little Nathanial knew about the school. "Rotating classes don't exist here. They divide the mind's attention. We take the same courses every day until we pass them."

"Oh." Nathanial was dismayed. That meant part of every day would be spent with the twisted teacher who had put him under the forget trick.

"Worried about Mr. Hutchince?" Juice asked.

"Eh, I'm sure it'll be fine." Nathanial shrugged.

"Don't count on it." Juice chortled unsympathetically.

"Yeah," Bee agreed, "looks like Mr. Hutchince has it out for you. He chooses someone every year and hadn't chosen his victim yet…until yesterday that is." She too had a cruel smile on her face.

"Thanks a lot for the words of comfort there, guys." Nathanial rolled his eyes. His group of supposed new friends all laughed. Aliya was obviously about to throw a fit on his behalf. Nathanial gave her the warning look and she swallowed her temper.

"What about tablets?" Nathanial asked, pondering another difference between the schools. He had used the Hyperion-provided tablet in his bedroom desk to talk to his mom, and he was very much aching to do so again. "Shouldn't we have them for taking class notes at least?"

"Tablets are a proven distraction from the learning process," Trid answered. "We have to remain completely submerged. No outside influences."

Nathanial tried not to let his inner dialogue show through what he hoped was an interested expression, but he couldn't believe how so many parents were allowing their children to be completely under Seizette's thumb. His mom would definitely not be happy if she knew the way Nathanial was being treated, and if he couldn't talk to her soon she would be sure to worry.

The school resonated and the sound of near a thousand students rising to their feet filled the vaulted space. The servers all lined up with their backs to the walls to let the pupils pass before they began to clean up.

The students were heading into the Factory Control classroom that was taught by Mr. Hutchince when Nathanial noticed Jerald standing by the entry.

"My lady requires your presence," Jerald said, hardly glancing at Nathanial.

"Who, me?" Nathanial pointed at himself and looked around at all the quizzical expressions. Everyone appeared desperate to know what was so special about him.

"Mmmyes." Jerald drawled it out as one single excruciating word.

After the uncomfortable walk through the hall of sprites forever petrified in sorrow, Nathanial found himself in the diamond office once again. This time the wall behind Seizette's desk had opened up to reveal gothic windows and the bright morning sunshine was beaming in past a vast rocky mountain landscape. Seizette herself was sitting at her desk and closing up a cylindrical device that appeared to encase a dozen shards of diamonds held aloft by bronze prongs. She stood up to reveal another exquisite and bedazzling dress the color of jade with elegant lace sleeves and a high neck, but her ebony hair was now pulled back into a long braid that reached past the middle of her back.

"Hello again, Nathanial. I hope you are finding the school enjoyable," Seizette said, and took a few steps around the desk to lean a curvaceous hip on its corner.

Jerald exited the room, shutting the door behind him.

"I wanted to speak with you about your place with us," she continued in her sultry tone. "But first I need to know how much your former caretakers have told you about… yourself."

Nathanial took a timid step closer and frowned. "I'm not sure what you mean."

"Well, surely they've mentioned how special you are. I don't see why they would want to keep that knowledge from you."

With a careful breath Nathanial considered Seizette. Was she trying to make him doubt his former companions? He already had trust issues without her comments. He had often wanted to see Boss as someone he could look up to, but the sprite's secretive ways always made him uncertain. Boss never liked to answer questions and often seemed to be using code when explaining himself.

"I'm not special," Nathanial finally said.

Seizette smiled warmly and pressed her hands together. She closed the space between them. "My dear Nathanial, you have always been special. Even when you were a human you did a great service to our kind with your unique immune deficiency." She saw Nathanial wince. "I know it was a great sacrifice of your freedom, to be locked up in that claustrophobic bedroom, but it was a beautiful sacrifice. Because of you, so many people prospered."

Nathanial sighed and looked away. He had to fight the building guilt that came with the image of the ghost town that Thatcherville had turned into after his wish to become a sprite was fulfilled. With his health, the hundreds of sprites who had worked to process his mucus into the popular multipurpose solution Grit the Gook were forced to pack up shop and move to greener pastures.

"Oh, look at you, darling," Seizette said, putting her smooth fingertips to his chin. He turned his eyes back onto her. "You feel remorse."

Then she pressed her fingers to her lips, as if she

could taste his feelings, and the taste was sweet.

"I want to offer you the chance to make an even greater difference to lives than you ever made as a factory," Seizette said with a twinkle in her eyes. "You are still special, but in a new way. Perhaps, with my help, we can make it a better way. Let me explain.

"Currently your human blood is battling with the sprite blood that is fighting to dominate your senses. The sprite pathways that allow you to feel the vibrations in the world are having to push past the human blockades that formed in your blood thousands of years ago, back when the humans branched off and away for the nature-attuned sprites. This can give you bursts of power that you will not know how to control. The turmoil is dangerous. If you do not choose a path quickly, figure out what kind of sprite you want to be, and concentrate the power through that path, the turmoil can rip you apart."

Nathanial felt momentarily faint and realized he had stopped breathing. Boss had mentioned something similar about his human and sprite vibrations being all jumbled up, but never mentioned any dangers.

"That is why this change has only been allowed to happen once before, and it was a very special circumstance at that. This happening again was a slip in the system, which I have now rectified. Furthermore, it was I who guided the first human who changed into a sprite, and therefore, only I who could possibly know what it will take to help you now. My work with the first changeling led to the man becoming a creature of such power that no one dared to reckon with him."

The vision of General Grantz flashed into Nathanial's mind. If he had been human, that would explain the battle blade. Only a human could wield a battle blade and only if a sprite had tapped it with power. Bunny had tapped his; Seizette must have done so for the general. Did Seizette know Nathanial had a battle blade strapped to his leg at that very moment?

"You're talking about General Grantz, aren't you?" Nathanial managed to get the words out from under the heavy burden of this news.

Seizette smiled and said, "You are quick, aren't you? Yes, and if it weren't for him we may never have convinced the rebels to sit down at the negotiating table. Many more lives would surely have been lost. Unfortunately, it seems that once a rebel, always a rebel, and they have been growing in numbers once again. There may soon be cause to defend our liberties.

"So you see, that is why I have decided to turn what seemed like a great loss to our people, the loss of your grand factory, into a fortuitous event. I will help you through this great change of yours, Nathanial. I believe it is the right thing to do.

"Now, I don't want to keep you from your classes for too long." She sashayed back over to her desk to swipe the tablet screen embedded in its surface. "I'm so glad we had this talk. I believe you can now feel confident in the choice you have made to join us."

The door opened and Jerald entered. Nathanial was considering those last words about choice. He'd only come here out of desperation to find Aliya, which wasn't much of a choice, and he felt like he was almost being blackmailed to stay now. Not only did he think fleeing may endanger the stop Seizette had put on Aliya's curse, but now he might also risk being ripped apart? What did that even mean?

"Uh, Miss—uh, Lady Seizette." Nathanial spoke hurriedly as Jerald's presence seemed to loom behind him. Seizette was taking her seat in a high-backed, velvety chair, but she looked up at him with mild interest. "You said I was the only one to go through this change after General Grantz, but, uh, didn't you just do the same thing to Aliya? Is she in danger of being ripped apart too?"

Seizette breathed a small laugh. "Oh, you are sweet, aren't you? Always worried for Aliya. You wear your heart on your sleeve." She licked her ruby lips as Nathanial's heartbeat quickened. "No," she finally said. "I did nothing to Aliya that she could not have done for herself. She is finally where she belongs." Seizette went back to occupying herself with the screen on her desk.

"I'm looking forward to great things from you, Nathanial," she called after him as Jerald ushered him out the door.

A Spy among Us

The buzz in Nathanial's mind was so preoccupying that he might as well have teleported back to the classroom. What did it all mean? That Aliya could have made herself a sprite, or was Seizette implying that Aliya had always been a sprite? That didn't make sense. She'd grown up in Israel. She had family there. Her mother died serving in the army because of the blood curse and Aliya had been afraid the curse would kill her and her sister the same way. Her sister…her sister hadn't been affected by the blood curse, that's what the wish sprite at the hearing had said. Should he tell Aliya? What would he say, exactly? He still didn't understand it himself.

Nathanial had barely taken a step into class when Mr. Hutchince halted his explanation of how to put a factory to sleep and looked directly at him. "You, come join me for this example."

Mr. Hutchince began swishing his palm an inch away from Nathanial's nose. He probably took longer to go to sleep than the teacher had anticipated, as he was concentrating on Seizette's words about being ripped apart rather than anything Mr. Hutchince was trying to do, but finally his brain was beginning to shut down and his head had started to tip down toward his chest when the walls vibrated. An echoing voice snapped Nathanial out of his haze.

"A compulsory assembly will now take place in the main courtyard. All teachers are to escort your students to their assigned balconies immediately." It sounded like Lady Seizette, and as her voice hadn't stopped echoing in his mind since he stood in her office, it was strange to hear it again so soon out loud.

Mr. Hutchince was thoroughly disappointed. He growled, saying, "You heard her: get out," and he stamped out of the room without fulfilling the obligation to lead his class.

The students rose chattering in excitement at the surprise assembly.

Nathanial found Aliya, Jozy, Trid, and the others in the hallway. They were playing a guessing game on what the assembly might be about. Bee was in the middle of saying something about an award being handed out when Juice cut in to say, "No, no, no. Lady Seizette prohibited awards years ago. No one gets recognition unless there's been an oath, and names don't even go in stone till next week."

"He's right," Trid added. "It's more likely to be a punishment, or a new set of rules. That's the only time we have assemblies anymore. Someone probably screwed up big time." He laughed.

Juice and Bee joined in Trid's amusement at the prospect of seeing a kid get punished. Aliya gawped at Nathanial, clearly saying, Can you believe these people?

They reached the bottommost balcony that made a rectangle around the hedgeball field. The field had been cleared of arches and the AstroTurf rolled up to reveal a black-and-red marble floor.

The rest of the school filed into overlooking positions in the balconies above. The students on each tier ascended in age from pale tweens at the bottom to older students ranging the entire spectrum of colors at the top.

Nathanial had learned that a sprite's color came with maturity and was determined by the blood classification that they usually inherited from their parents. He wondered what color he might be when his time came, seeing as he didn't have sprite parents. But he also knew it was possible to change one's color. If a sprite studied hard enough they could change their blood trait, like his friend Bunny. She had been born a wish sprite but had learned, or was learning, to be a dust sprite. He hadn't even started training for a particular trait yet. Swartza High probably didn't offer such training. That could be unique to Hyperion; a lot seemed to be special there. He really did miss that place.

With a thoughtful smile, Nathanial began to imagine what it might be like to go to school there again, and really give it his all this time. Maybe, if the plan worked, he would get to go back. The thought was unsettling, but in an exciting sort of way. He'd been sure he wanted to go back to his normal human school, with his normal human friends, but then he thought of Mila, the punk-rock sprite with attitude who had helped him get through his days and set out to save Aliya. He had grown to trust her and rely on her, and he even missed her. It was even more funny how much he missed Spassel, a quirky little sprite who wanted nothing more than to be Nathanial's friend, and who had big dreams of changing his color and going into politics.

Nathanial's eyebrows furrowed as he contemplated Spassel. Hadn't he said his parents were yellow and so he probably would be too when he grew up? The servants at Swartza High were all yellow. Could that have been why he was so embarrassed to say it? Was his class of sprites expected to serve others?

A bright light filled the room at that moment, and once his vision cleared, Nathanial saw Lady Seizette standing on a platform in the center of the arena. She had changed out of her dress and into a uniquely beautiful business suit, with diamonds running along its seams. Her silky black hair was twisted up into diamond combs.

The entire courtyard hushed.

"Thank you all for being so quick and orderly," she began, speaking smoothly and clearly. She had no microphone but it was as though she were speaking right in front of him. "I have called you all here to bear witness to the capture of an intruder."

Everyone around Nathanial looked excited; everyone but Aliya and Jozy.

"He was found in the kitchens, attempting to poison our afternoon meal. He is a rebel and a spy."

Two large uniformed sprites escorted a small figure with a bag over his head into the center of the room. Nathanial was shocked at how tiny the kicking sprite was. How could this be a rebel and a spy?

"This is further proof of what we already knew, that the rebels will stoop to anything in hopes to shake our strong foundation. And so for the crimes against the Swartza and affiliation with the treacherous filth, I sentence this rebel to a series of reconditionings through the diamond. If within the course of this year it disowns its rebel allegiance and agrees to a life of servitude, to which it was born, it will be free to take up such a life. If reconditioning does not take, and it continues to fight its nature, it will be within the diamond's keep for one decade before reconditioning will be reattempted."

Lady Seizette pulled the black bag off the young sprite's head and asked, "Does it understand?"

Nathanial gasped. It was Spassel!

AN ACCOUNT OF THE CROSSING TREATY

Spassel stood shivering and blinking up at Lady Seizette. "I'm n-not a sp-spy," he managed to say.

"Who and what it is are known. A simple yes or no is required now. Does it understand its punishment?" Lady Seizette asked coldly.

Spassel whimpered, "Y-yes."

Students around the stadium were amused at Spassel's pain. Trid laughed softly beside Nathanial; and he could not stand it. His arm was in punching position without a thought, aiming for Trid's head, but Aliya locked her elbow around his and pulled him back behind the crowd.

"What are you doing? Schmoozing required, remember?" she whispered frantically.

Nathanial was having a hard time thinking straight. His anger hadn't boiled over like this since Cyron ripped Aliya away from him, and he'd raised his fists on that occasion too.

"I know him," Nathanial said, eyes searching the arena for a route down to Spassel. "He's my friend."

Aliya put her hand on Nathanial's cheek and forced him to look at her. "I'm sorry, Nathan, but there's nothing you can do right now."

"I have to do something." He trembled.

"I know, but not right now."

Nathanial caught Trid looking at him. "What are you doing? This is the best part," Trid said, ushering them back to the ledge.

Nathanial and Aliya timidly looked again over the balcony. Lady Seizette had her hands on Spassel's shoulders. His skin was glowing and crystalizing. Diamonds grew out from Spassel's pores and an expression of agonizing pain formed upon his screaming face until the sound was suffocated into silence.

Aliya put her hand over her mouth in shock. Nathanial wanted to shout out for them to stop but he dug his nails deep into the wood of the banister to contain himself.

Spassel was soon completely encased within a block of diamond. Lady Seizette removed her hands from the crystal as if it were a pail of water. The students began to applaud. She smiled, her perfect teeth sparkling up at them.

"Let this be a reminder," Seizette began again when the crowd had calmed down. "Our enemy still spawns. They are growing in number and they spread their lies young. But age makes no difference in the strong faces I see here before me either. You are the next generation of defenders of what those who came before you accomplished through sacrifice and belief. One day soon you too may have to fight for our liberty, our abilities, and our birthright to become all that we can be without restraint, without hiding, and without being told we are the weaker creatures. We are the strong!"

The students burst into applause, cheers, and whistles. Aliya and Nathanial looked at each other wide-eyed, both thinking the same thing. That speech sounded like a captain addressing her troops before battle.

There was another blinding light from where Seizette stood, and when it was gone, so were she and Spassel.

"Where'd he go?" Nathanial asked, leaning precariously over the edge of the balcony.

"What?" Trid asked, backing away with the rest of the dispersing students.

"The—the block of diamond. Where is it?" Nathanial asked.

"I don't know." Trid shrugged. "No one knows

where Lady Seizette keeps her victims." He chuckled.

Nathanial wanted to wring Trid's throat just then, which meant it was Aliya's turn to shoot him a warning look. He wasn't sure he could schmooze with this creep after all. He needed to find out where the diamonds were kept. But wait, he'd seen Aliya being pulled out of the diamond in Seizette's office! That had to be the access point. He wasn't sure he could get there on his own; he had always had Jerald to guide him before. Where would Jerald be right now?

Nathanial was so distracted during bio-modifications class that he was no help in transmogrifying the roly-poly with the beetle. Everyone came out of that class covered in goop. This of course left Trid annoyed with him during weapons training and he purposefully cut every bit of Nathanial he could reach. But finally it was lunch and Nathanial hoped to spot Jerald. He kept peering over all the tables until Trid punched the leafy bandage that covered his shoulder.

"Seriously, Nat, what is your problem? You've been skunking up all day."

Nathanial was ready to give Trid what for when he caught himself. If he was going to have to socialize with this smug, cold-hearted sprite, it was time he got something out of it. Besides that, even if he freed Spassel he would still need the escape plan to be set up.

"Sorry, Trid, I've just been thinking about taking the diamond oath and it's made me all fidgety."

"Really!" Trid perked up. "Why didn't you say so, spit? Do you know who you are talking to here?"

"Yeah, I do." Nathanial put on his best admiring stare. "I just didn't know how to go about asking you for advice."

"I can understand that. Technically I can't tell you any of the details. The Diamond Trials have to be kept secret. But I can make sure you'll pass."

"Seriously! That'd be nectar, Trid!" Nathanial had heard a few sprites use nectar where he'd usually say cool. It seemed to do the trick. Trid was smiling more smugly than ever.

Nathanial looked over to Aliya who was smiling proudly down at her mashed potatoes. She had picked all the flower petals out. There was always some strange little twist like that to sprite food, but at least breads, chopped fruits, and potatoes were used often enough to keep Aliya from starving.

Trid was much easier to deal with for the rest of the day. He was actually being nice, in a genuine way. The usual phony smile with an undertone of sinister was replaced with honest encouragement.

During hedgeball, Trid showed Nathanial how to pick the strongest hedgehogs. The trick was to whisper "Cat!" in their ear, and if they did not shed a quill, then they were good to go.

Then, during dinner, Trid told Nathanial how to get Mr. Hutchince off his back. Supposedly, Mr. Hutchince had once been up for Lady Seizette's position, and in order to stop him from competing with her she removed his heart. Nathanial couldn't believe this literally but continued to listen as Trid advised him to tell Mr. Hutchince how Lady Seizette had handpicked him for Swartza High and she personally wanted to thank him for being so taken with Nathanial. The idea was that Mr. Hutchince would back off if he knew messing with Nathanial was basically asking for more punishment from Seizette. Nathanial thought it sounded like he'd be treading on thin ice to say such a thing, but it was good to have the information in case of an emergency.

Trid's greatest gesture of kindness came as they were walking down the dorm hallway at the end of the day. Nathanial was about to go into his room when Trid said, "Wait, I was going to show you my room, remember?"

Nathanial put on a fake smile and followed Trid a few doors down. He wasn't sure how much longer he could suffer this sweet side of the boy. It was enough to give him a toothache.

They went into Trid's room. It was similar to Nathanial's but without a balcony as it was on the opposite side of the hall. Instead, his window looked out onto a play yard, the very one where they had weapons training. The canopy bed was thick green marble and the draperies matched the tone. The couches and chairs were a bit cushier than Nathanial's but the mattress seemed very firm.

Nathanial went to test this theory by pushing his fist into it. It was indeed stiff and that reminded him to ask, "Does your bed throw you out in the mornings?"

Trid laughed. "No, I hate that. I've told my windows to open at sunrise. The morning air is enough to get me out of bed."

"Humph." Nathanial thought. "Good idea. So I'll just switch the tap, then," he said, testing his guess.

"Yeah," Trid said, only half listening. He was occupied opening a dresser drawer and pulling out a large leather-bound book. He brought it over to Nathanial. "This is all you'll need to learn if you are going to pass the trials."

Nathanial took the book and immediately

became excited. "The Crossing Treaty," he read the title out loud.

"I know what you're thinking. Everyone knows about the Crossing Treaty, but I assure you, you've never heard the story the way that book tells it. My grandfather wrote it. He was there."

Nathanial looked up at Trid in surprise. This was too much. "I can't take this. Your grandfather wrote it? It has to stay with you." Nathanial tried to hand it back.

"I'm not giving it to you, just read it. But don't tell anyone about it. It's a trade secret. You can return it after you've passed the trials." Trid winked.

"Why are you sharing this with me?" Nathanial asked, not believing Trid capable of selflessness.

Trid narrowed his eyes, clearly wondering how much to say. "I know there's something about you, Nat. Lady Seizette doesn't let just anyone into this school. I can't tell you the last time someone not of the century bloodline was taught here. I'm hoping she's right about you, and that we can be friends."

Nathanial gulped then tried to smile. "I don't know what to say. Thanks."

Trid put a hand on Nathanial's shoulder with a smile. "Sure thing, spit. Now go start reading! You'll put your name in stone next week and you can take the trials soon after. I know you can do it."

Nathanial turned toward the door then looked back to ask, "What if I don't pass?"

Trid shook his head, saying, "If you don't come out of the trials then that's it. You just don't come out."

With those words Nathanial took his leave. In the safety of his bedroom he plopped down face-first into a pillow and moaned loudly. He felt the overwhelming weight of potential failure crushing in on him. The responsibility to free his friends, himself, and some disembodied voice that he'd begun to think was a hallucination was proving to be too much.

Rolling over, he took a breath and remembered the words from a book on "taming anxiety" he had read back in his old bedroom. Take it one step at a time was the best advice from those pages. Books had always been an escape for him before and this Crossing Treaty book could lead to his literal escape now.

Nathanial rubbed the leathery words on the thick cover. He'd been curious about the Crossing Treaty ever since Boss had first mentioned it. He knew it had something to do with the breaking of the bond between sprites and humans. Before it, sprites could openly negotiate with humans, but after it, they were never even allowed to let a human know they existed. This was actually worse for the human, as sprites continued to use them as factories, taking whatever they needed from them without returning any favors. Nathanial and Aliya had both been factories, abused factories, to the point that they had made wishes ten years long to break their factory status.

With the flipping of the first page, Nathanial knew it was going to be a tough read. Trid wasn't kidding when he said his grandfather had written it. The words were in black, scratchy, hand-scribbled ink! Nathanial turned back to the first page and read:

An account of the Crossing Treaty

By: Captain Whirlvauhl Brunt

There was a bust sketch of the captain beneath his name. He wore a large hat that was curved up on one side and he had a twisted mustache that appeared to be tipped with cactus needles.

Nathanial took the book firmly in his hands to quickly scan the hundreds of pages as they flipped through the air. He suddenly stopped the cascade and turned back a short way. There was a two-page diagram of a battle. Upon a hill, raised up high and posed just like he still was in the piece of diamond, was the general and his monstrous transmogrified winged bear. Dozens of bodies were flying away from a swatting paw.

Nathanial thought he was going to leave the book for reading on the weekend, as classes had left him exhausted, but the pictures kept him turning the pages. There were sketches and watercolor paintings of weapons, plants with medical attributes, potions and poisons, and people being punished; lots of people being punished. Nathanial looked for a long time at one in particular before he decided to read what the passage had to say on it.

The greatest fighter among the opposition could not only out-wield our best swordsman three times over, but his charisma and fine words had people switching sides by the flock. In the end it was not the assassins we sent for him, *or the wall of guards between him and our citadel that brought him down, but our very own Queen of Crusades.*

He had come to bring her down himself, but with a single touch she ensnared his heart and sapped his will. She stripped him of title and color; in a flash he had no idea what he had been fighting for.

Nathanial looked again at the depiction of the sprite being stripped of his title and color. On the left stood a tall, strong orange sprite in armor, a proud look on his face and a sword held high. On the right, the sprite was transformed, his figure hunched with shame and despair. He was in rags, he had become blue in color...and he was undoubtedly the sprite whose job it had been to keep human Nathanial sick, and who had then whisked him off to a wish hearing where he became a sprite. This man had guided him to Hyperion to be taught the sprite ways, trained him in swordplay, and somewhere along the way, became his unlikely friend and mentor.

"Boss," Nathanial whispered. He recalled a petri sprite commenting on Boss's color change once. He'd recognized Boss, no matter how much Boss denied it. Could it have been from the third rebellion? How was that possible? Trid's grandfather had written this book. How old would that have to make Boss? But then again, how old was Seizette? He had heard that sprites lived lengthy lives but this was getting ridiculous.

Nathanial could not stop after that. Page after page he read. He discovered that the petri sprites had allied with the Swartza. They used their petrification ability to turn hundreds of the enemy into stone at the queen's command. The drawings looked very much the same as the figures he had seen frozen in the halls throughout the school.

He learned that the Skilla had played both sides but their loyalty was to the rebels. Because of their successful infiltration they were able to warn the public and stop the passing of many cleverly worded laws, one of which would imprison any sprite whose view differed from the queen's. Nathanial remembered his Skilla friend,

Mila, saying, "Because of the Skilla we have our freedoms." No way could Nathanial stop reading after that, no matter how dry his eyes were getting.

The book did not only give gory details about the brutality involved in the events leading up to the Crossing Treaty, often referred to as the third rebellion, but also explicit instructions on how to perform some of the most complicated tricks for gaining control over the enemy. Nathanial excitedly pulled out the notebook that Boss had bought him, and began recording useful information; the golden words on the cover, Everything I need to know is within, seemed to become more accurate with every entry he made. But as he let the self-writing glass pen copy down one of the several tricks he thought could be helpful in his upcoming trials, a warming sensation grew against his chest until: "Ouch!"

Nathanial pulled the necklace Mila had given him out from under his shirt. Its metallic swirls glowed red-hot.

"Guess you're done for the night," Nathanial said to the necklace.

He hoped the necklace's response meant that he'd be able to do all the tricks he had just read about! If so, maybe he could pass the trials after all.

Feeling more at ease about the situation, Nathanial put the book into his bedside table drawer. For the first time in ages, when his head hit the pillow he fell sound asleep.

STEP UP TO STEP ONE

Unfortunately, Nathanial had forgotten to command his bed not to yank him out of the sheets in the morning. He screamed, then steadied himself and stood there at the foot of his bed in momentary waking confusion. Then he turned right around to his bed and said, "Don't do that again!"

But he knew he'd have to do more than that. He placed his hand on the post, found the bed's vibrations and gave the order again. He could sense the vibrations running from the bedpost into the floor and all around the room so he added, "And while you're at it, tell the windows they have your job from now on! Just have them open this time in the mornings and close again when I leave the room." He paused as his temper waned and thought he should add, "Thank you," in case they took offense to his short tone.

This being only Nathanial's third day at the school, he was amazed at how quickly he'd settled into a routine and become comfortable with the flow of his day. Breakfast, evil teacher class, splice some bugs together, kick some butt at sword fighting, lunch, play a twisted version of horse polo, shower, food again, then bed. But bedtime now gave him something exciting to look forward to every night. Something that led him closer to getting out of there: reading The Crossing Treaty! He studied it every night until his necklace burned before the weekend came to break things up.

It was Saturday morning and the most unusual thing happened: nothing. His windows had burst open every previous day since his command but this morning Nathanial just opened his eyes naturally. The Crossing Treaty book was still open on his pillow. A picture of an ice sprite deflecting a fire sprite's ball of flame still gleamed from its pages.

Nathanial sat up and smiled. Instead of a school uniform he put on a sprite version of jeans and a T-shirt; in this case the shimmery blue button-up collared shirt with dark velvety crisscrosses and the pair of loose-fit brown pants that had so many different types of pockets they appeared to be scavenged from multiple outfits. He had bought these clothes using some money Boss had given him to go shopping with at the Hyperion market. Sprite styles were often patched together with more than one kind of fabric. It was like wearing a less intense version of a patchwork quilt. Sprites liked to make things out of various different bits, but they did it with style.

Nathanial had been told the dining hall would serve all day on weekends, so there was no rush to get to meals, and his door would be open, allowing him to come and go as he pleased. He could do pretty much anything that he liked, except go outside of course. Kids would usually meet in the swimming pool yard or at the hedgeball field. Since Aliya and Nathanial had yet to see the pool yard they'd agreed to meet there after they ate at their own convenience.

Nathanial realized what a late riser he was when no one he recognized was at breakfast. He ate quickly and was trying to follow the route to the pool yard that Jozy had explained to him when he felt shivers run down his spine again.

"Nathanial." The faint voice echoed around him.

Nathanial looked around the brightly lit passage. Diamond veins dominated the volcanic walls and a high circular window allowed the sun's rays to stream in, but there was not a soul in sight.

"Who are you?" Nathanial asked into empty air. "Are you a ghost?"

"Nathanial," the voice called again, louder. "Over here."

Nathanial had worked out which direction the voice was coming from now, and turned to a large diamond vein next to him. He could see a shape within it but the features were indiscernible.

"I see you," Nathanial said, stepping closer. "Who are you?"

"You barely know me, Nathanial Thatcher, but I helped you once. I need your help now," the voice said sorrowfully.

"I'd be happy to help you. I just don't know how. What do you need me to do?"

"I was once a crystal grower, but I had changed my color," the voice explained. "A remnant of who I was is still within me. That is how I can speak to you now, but I am not as powerful as she. I need you to go to her office and take the diamond key from her desk."

"Lady Seizette's desk?"

"Yes. She has a key that she allows others, like her captain, to use, so that a non-crystal sprite may access the diamond."

"You're trapped in the diamond. Of course! Do you see Spassel in there?" Nathanial asked, quickly becoming excited.

The voice was silent and the vague form faded

away.

"Wait, please. My friend is trapped in there too." Nathanial put his hand where her form had been but she did not return.

Nathanial backed away, his excitement fading. He now knew there was a way to free Spassel, but getting into Lady Seizette's office would not be easy. The escape plan would still need to be ready to go as well, and he had to pass the trials for that. Then there was the matter of the escapees having increased in number from two to four. Would Sidian be able to carry four sprites? Surely he was big enough, Nathanial tried to convince himself.

Just then a shadow passed over the high windows in the hall and a sound like an electric shock crackled within the walls. Nathanial jumped in fright and ran from the area.

He hurried on toward the pool, wanting to tell Aliya all that had just happened. He hadn't mentioned the voice to her before now, as it hadn't returned and he'd thought it might never do so, but now that it was real, and had apparently helped him, he needed her advice.

Nathanial found Aliya having a carefree chat with Jozy, lying back in some comfy chairs in the courtyard by the pool. He hated to pull her away, but it couldn't wait.

"I agree," she said after listening to Nathanial's urgent ramble about possible courses of action. "You need to pass the trials before you free your friends from the diamond, but it wouldn't hurt to work on a plan for getting into Seizette's office. I've been there before, when she turned me. I saw the desk."

"Was it in a room with a big flower vase on a coffee table and diamonds splitting through the walls?"

"Yes."

"Then I've seen it too. That's where she pulled you out of the walls and where I met her again for that terrible chat about me possibly being her next General Grantz." Nathanial felt a twinge at the memory. He hadn't told Aliya everything about that conversation, like how she was somehow a sprite in a different way than him, but it wasn't like he was hiding anything. How could he explain something that he didn't understand himself?

"I was in the diamond?" Aliya asked, surprised.

Nathanial nodded. "That's how Malik learned about you, I think. It sounds like when you're in the diamond it kind of downloads your memories. Seizette says it's intelligent, and the trapped girl says Malik can access it using a key."

Aliya shivered. "Creepy."

"Do you remember how to get to the office?"

"Maybe, but I'm not sure. Jerald escorted me to and from there."

"Yeah, I've been looking for him all week. What does he do when he's not moving kids around?"

"Not sure." Aliya groaned. "But I doubt he would take us just because we asked him to. Maybe Jozy knows how to get there."

Nathanial looked sideways toward Jozy. She was watching them but quickly feigned disinterest at Nathanial's notice of her. "Do you really trust her that much?"

"Yes," Aliya stated confidently.

"Well, let's not ask her just yet. I have an idea about Jerald and I think I could convince him if I could just find him. We can't even attempt a rescue until after the trials anyway."

"Okay," Aliya said, nodding. "And what about that electric sound you heard? Was it the same sound that we heard before Malik stopped us getting on that balcony?"

"Yeah, I don't know. It's weird, right? Maybe it's something to do with the diamonds growing in the walls. Maybe it takes power or something."

"Could be. There's so much we don't know about this place." Aliya bit her lip, then asked interestedly, "How's the reading going?"

"Good!" Nathanial smiled. He had been keeping her up to date on everything he learned from the book whenever they had a solitary moment, and even let her read his personal journal, having realized he had never properly told her about his ten-year wish. He hadn't shared it before because of the rule that would nullify his wish if he told it to anyone else, and these days he just didn't have time. But it didn't seem fair that he knew so much about her, having attended her hearing, and she knew so little about him. He wanted her to know everything. She had been thankful to him for sharing something so personal and he felt they were closer for it. It was also nice that he could teach her some new things about the sprites after all she had taught him from Mataunte's stories, and this latest info was sure to tickle her. "Just learned how to deflect a fire sprite's flame. Wish we'd known that trick a year ago, huh?" He chuckled.

"Well, for me that seems like only a few days ago, but even so we couldn't do sprite tricks. We were humans, remember?"

"Oh right." Nathanial scrunched up his nose.

Aliya laughed. "But you'll still have to teach me how it's done." She paused. "Do you think we will ever be human again?"

Nathanial sighed. "I don't know if that's possible.

Do you want to be?"

Aliya appeared appalled, as if the question was abominable. Then she looked over to Jozy and back to Nathanial with sad eyes. "I—I guess I—I don't know anymore," she finally said with a huge exhale. "If I thought my family were waiting for me then I would say yes, absolutely, but they must surely think I'm dead and have long since mourned me. I also don't know how I would explain to them that I haven't aged. I just don't know. I do miss them, but I can also see the appeal of being a sprite, if we could use our abilities for good and not for domination, I mean. Maybe I could help my people in some way."

"I know what you mean," Nathanial said. "It's kind of like having superpowers. They can be awesome when used the right way. When we get out of here, I could take you to Hyperion. It's an amazing school. There are more sprites like Jozy there. Really good-hearted sprites who want to do right by the factories. It's more like that symbiotic relationship you were talking about, when the sprites and humans first lived together."

"What about your mom? Have you told her anything, you know, about being a sprite?"

"Not really. She thinks I'm away on some kind of exchange program. When I knew I'd be coming to look for you, I told her I wasn't sure when next I could call but that was over a couple of weeks ago. I hope she isn't too worried. I miss her a lot; but Aliya, about your family: it's been, what, six years since you saw them? That's a long time, but it's not a lifetime. We should tell your family you're still alive. We can make something up to cover your young appearance, or even better, we can probably put some kind of trick on their eyes to make you look a little older, then we'll tell them the same exchange program story as mine and we can go to Hyperion together. We'll see our families when school's out!"

Hope shone in Aliya's eyes. "Do you really think so?"

Nathanial's heart seemed to fill with helium as her smile lifted his spirits. He nodded to say, "I know so."

Nathanial spent most of the rest of the day with Aliya and Jozy, happily lounging by the pool, eating sweets as they passed by the food hall, and practicing funny tricks on each other. Jozy showed them how to conjure up a burp so long they could say the alphabet and Nathanial tried out a foot-tingling trick he'd read in the Crossing Treaty book that made Aliya kick in such a funny way that they laughed for what seemed like a half an hour.

It was all going so well until Trid showed up. "There you guys are," he said, approaching with Bee and Juice on each side of him. "Thought we were meeting at the pool after lunch?"

"Breakfast," Jozy cleared up. "We said we were going this morning and we did."

"Oh, misunderstanding, then." Trid smiled. "Anyway, I'm glad I found you, Nat. It's time to sign you up for the trials."

"Already?" Nathanial gulped.

"Indeed," Trid said, putting his arm around Nathanial, and escorted him away from the others.

"But I haven't finished the book," Nathanial said.

"You'll still have time, I'm sure. Signing up just informs Lady Seizette who is interested. She picks a student off the list every other day or so. The likelihood you will be first is very slim."

The dread built up in Nathanial like a snowball growing into an avalanche. The book was hundreds of pages long and he'd maybe got through a third of it; and that was with skipping around a lot.

Trid showed Nathanial into a room with a vaulted ceiling, like a miniature version of the dining hall. But instead of tables there were two rows of impressive statues in fighting stance, and between them at least a hundred colorful teenage students were filing toward a table in the distance.

"This is where I leave you, my friend. Good luck," Trid said, patting Nathanial on the back, and left him wavering at the tail end of the snaking line.

Nathanial squirmed with unease. He was shorter than anyone else in that room and the only one who hadn't found his color yet. It was embarrassing. Many of the sprites had spotted him and were whispering to each other.

It took half an hour before the line shortened enough for Nathanial to make out what the sprites at the front were doing. A block of diamond sat on a table and as each sprite approached they would put their hand on it, pull a face that suggested they were enduring pain, and finally jerk their hand free again, as if it'd been stuck in tar. Unfortunately the proceedings were headed by a tall, stern sprite, who Nathanial recognized as Captain Malik. The nerves at the sight of him made Nathanial feel nauseous.

As Nathanial's turn approached he was feeling light-headed, and every possible retreat scenario was running through his mind. The problem was every one of them ended with him trapped in diamond, Aliya yelling at his stone block for not going through with the plan, Trid calling him a coward, and poor Spassel frozen next to him with the ghostly voice forever echoing her disappointment at him. So, there was only one thing for it: he needed to pull himself together and look up into those eyes that he loathed.

"Nathanial. What a surprise," said Captain Malik, raising his eyebrows.

"Yeah." Nathanial swallowed. "I bet it is."

Captain Malik narrowed his piercing eyes. Nathanial wondered if he was trying to read the plan in his mind, and thought he'd better hurry before the sprite succeeded. He put his right hand onto the five-fingered indention scooped into the diamond's surface. Pins and needles prickled his palm. He saw his name being carved into the diamond just above his middle finger in the style of his own handwriting.

As the final r of his last name was completed, the pain in his palm intensified as if the little needles had grown into massive swords. When he yanked his hand free he was amazed it was still whole. He watched his name sink into the crystal, wondering how the block wasn't soaked in blood, then with a last hateful glance at Captain Malik's glowering eyes he turned away and rushed past the queue behind him.

Not until he reached the empty hallway did Nathanial clasp his right hand in his left and exclaim, "Oouuch!" The pain suggested a giant gash in his flesh, and despite what his eyes saw his mind refused to believe nothing was there. After flexing his fingers and shaking his hand continuously for a while, Nathanial tried putting it between his forearm and side. The constant pressure seemed to help.

Just then a figure crossed the end of the hall. At the sight, Nathanial momentarily forgot his pain and ran down to the fork in the passage. He saw the figure turn a corner.

"Wait," Nathanial called and made a dash for it. When he rounded the end of the passage he ran smack-dab into his prey. Apparently Jerald had heard Nathanial and stopped to wait for him.

"Can I help you?" the yellow sprite asked with a drawl.

"Jerald," Nathanial gasped with a laugh. "It's so good to see you."

Jerald looked surprised. "Really?" Then he looked to Nathanial's side. "What is wrong with your hand?"

Nathanial removed it from its cradled position. "Oh, nothing. I wanted to ask if you could direct me to Lady Seizette's office."

Jerald's surprised expression intensified to the point that his eyebrows became lost in his yellow bangs. "Why ever would you want to go there?"

"Well, I really don't want to, but I have to, see?" Nathanial licked his lips, hoping his idea was going to work. "You know that boy that she put in diamond a few days ago? Well, he's my friend. And if you could direct me to her office, I think I could help him." Nathanial held his breath and waited to see if Jerald's expression changed in his favor.

"Your friend," Jerald finally said, his eyebrows falling. "How odd. It was said he is a spy."

"He's not a spy, and I think you know that," Nathanial said seriously.

The thing was Nathanial knew that adult sprites were in tune with sprite youths and could tell what they would grow up to be. The Crossing Treaty book had reminded him of this when a passage described how the Swartza would sort through orphaned children. Those with the traits they desired would be assistants to generals. The rest would clean the stables or fetch the provisions.

Nathanial knew that Jerald and Spassel were the same, and that Jerald would have sensed it at the assembly. Now he just had to hope that Jerald wasn't truly loyal to the Swartza, that he only worked for them, and just maybe he didn't even have a choice about it.

Jerald had been silent for long enough to make Nathanial uncomfortable when he finally said, "I don't know anything of the sort, and neither do you if you know what is good for you."

Nathanial's heart fell. Jerald turned to walk away

"But," Jerald said in a hardly audible tone, "all anyone would have to do to find the office of a diamond queen would be to follow the growing diamonds."

Jerald continued down the hall without a glance behind him. Nathanial smiled.

THE OATH

Nathanial hurried back toward his room, determined to get through as much of the Crossing Treaty book as he could. He glanced into Aliya's room on passing and was surprised to see her sitting alone on her bed. He turned back and poked his head through the door.

"Hey! Whatcha' doin' in here all by your lonesome? Where's Jozy?"

Aliya laughed. "I do like to be by myself occasionally, Nathan."

"Oh." He wasn't sure if that was a hint. "Should I leave you alone?"

"No! You have to tell me what happened with the trial sign-up sheet. Get over here, silly!"

Nathanial jogged in. "It wasn't a sheet at all," he said, slumping down next to her, and held out the hand that had felt such pain, though he didn't even have a rash to prove it. He explained the torturous event in great detail and only became excited when he got to the part about running into Jerald, literally. "I think I know what he means, too," Nathanial continued. "Diamonds grow all over this school but if you noticed there are some hallways where they get really big! I was in one the other day that was about ninety percent diamond. I bet I was close to the office then."

"Yeah, there were definitely some diamond hallways on the way there. It makes sense," Aliya said, nodding. "That was pretty gutsy, what you did."

"What?" Nathanial asked.

"Telling Jerald you were Spassel's friend. He could have turned you in."

"I guess so. I just had a feeling about him, you know. I can tell Jerald doesn't like it here. None of the yellow servants do. Look how they're treated."

"I know. It's sad."

Nathanial sighed. "Anyway, I better get back to my homework. I have a lot of reading to do if I'm going to pass these trials."

"I wonder what the trials are going to be."

"I have no idea. I'm trying to read all the tricks in the book first. That's most likely to be of use I'd think. I don't know how the history of the Crossing Treaty itself will do anything for me but it's definitely interesting stuff."

"Good luck," Aliya said as Nathanial headed toward the door.

"Thanks," he said, waving as he exited.

Over the rest of the weekend Nathanial felt he was getting a good handle on the tricks in the book. Fainting, tripping, sneezing, wheezing, twitching, and choking were just a few of the tricks the Swartza used to mess up an oncoming attacker, and each of them was described in detail.

On Monday night Nathanial decided to start back at the beginning and read how the rebellion arose in the first place. The book had been written with an obvious bias for the Swartza, and made it sound like a bunch of never-happy-unless-complaining sprites started the feud by accusing certain political groups of gaining unfair amounts of wealth and power through the misuse of factories. Sides were formed, with those who felt cheated opposing those who supported the monarchy. As the disgruntled grew in number and battles began to be waged, a compromise had to be reached before the entire civilization tore itself apart. That was when the Crossing Treaty was signed and the council was formed. It was made up half of elected officials and half of the old ruling class known as the century families. Seizette had had to step down from her position as queen.

The Crossing Treaty was the end to a third rebellion in their history. The first one having been when the humans left faery and the second when Lady Seizette had come into power as queen in the first place. She had restored order and regained some semblance of control over the chaos that the splintering groups had caused. At that time she was revered as a great leader who had brought them back from the brink of extinction and turned them into one of the dominant species on the planet. It was no wonder she had such strong support if this was true, but it appeared that after such a long reign the power had gone to her head. The sprites having surpassed the disappearing races of elves, goblins, and fairies, she was soon on the warpath to send the humans into the realm of myth as well. Nathanial was thankful, to say the least, that she was no longer in a position to carry out that plan.

It wasn't until Wednesday, during weapons training, that the first sprite was called for the trials. The class was learning how to wield an axe when Nathanial was distracted by Lady Seizette's voice and he nearly got his head chopped off.

"I'm proud to announce that our first great defender has entered the trials on his journey of worthiness. May he venture true as our founders did and come out victorious, having earned his right to take the oath."

The class applauded after the announcement. Nathanial felt a knot in his stomach along with the now all-too-common ache in his back.

"Are you about to sprout, or what, Nat?" Trid asked, watching Nathanial flexing his shoulder blades.

"What?" Nathanial lifted an eyebrow.

"Well, you're a fay, right? Don't your kind sprout about now? You've sure been acting like you're going to."

Nathanial shrugged like he knew what they were talking about. "It's probably about time."

Trid lifted his axe, preparing to spar again. "You better hope you do it soon and learn how to use them before the trials, or hope you don't get them until after. I wouldn't want to sprout during. Then again I wouldn't want to sprout at all. Too much hassle for my liking."

Nathanial lifted his eyebrows. He'd heard that before. Were they talking about wings? How on earth did you handle wings? If only Boss were there. He had wings, he'd know if Nathanial were going to sprout. But as there was nothing he could actually do, Nathanial chose to slip into denial. It was probably just a backache from slouching too much. He wasn't going to get wings. That was just silly!

Hours went by without another announcement. Kids were starting to take bets on whether the sprite who was taking the trials would ever resurface.

Nathanial was finishing up his dinner of scalloped maggots when a tall smoke-colored teen in his school uniform stepped into the hall accompanied by Lady Seizette. She looked royal; her sparkling dress with a high whisk collar trailed a foot behind her. Her hair was braided over her shoulder and adorned with jewels. Everyone hushed and stared at her.

Nathanial had expected the student to look proud but instead he had no expression. Seizette on the other hand looked proud as a peacock. The two walked up to the diamond-studded throne that sat atop several marble steps at the end of the room. Seizette sat down and the small train of her dress wrapped around her feet. The teen knelt in front of her.

"Is he about to be knighted, or what?" Nathanial couldn't help but ask.

Bee shushed him from behind as lady Seizette addressed the adoring crowd.

"You, Jester Hornsby the Fifth, have passed the trials, making proud your family this day, and too, your Lady Seizette, who may no longer be queen in title but hopefully is still queen in your heart."

She looked up to the students with a glistening red smile and the crowd chanted in unison, "A diamond queen, a people's queen, and always the queen of our hearts. Lady Seizette."

Lady Seizette held up her hands and diamonds began to grow in them. They took shape as they extended twice the length of each arm and for the first time Nathanial noticed more detail in them. One formed into a key, with the world globe atop it, and the other was a key topped by a heart with a crown shining in its center. She brought them both down to cross one another then rested them on the teen's shoulders so his neck was at their intersection.

Then she put her hands palm up to watch a great diamond sword form in them. But this couldn't be right, Nathanial thought: Why would she be placing the tip at the boy's heart, one hand under the shaft for support, the other making its way to the hilt as if for a thrust? Was she about to commit murder in front of the entire school? Nathanial felt himself rising and watching in horror as the sword tip began to enter the boy's chest.

"What is she doing?" Nathanial asked in disbelief.

Trid pulled him quickly back down.

Nathanial was ready to resist when he realized the sword was entering as easily as a blade through butter. There was no blood but instead a soft warm glow where the sword began to be absorbed into the boy's chest.

"Do you, Jester Hornsby the Fifth, swear to uphold the honor of your people?" Seizette asked smoothly.

"I swear it," answered the teen and in response the sword was pushed in farther.

"And do you swear to be resilient in the face of all adversaries who rebel against our cause?"

"I swear it." He only gave the slightest hint of feeling any pressure as the sword was pushed still farther in.

"Do you swear to protect your queen when those who wish to harm her come upon our gates?"

"I swear it." The sword was halfway in now, with no sign of it exiting the other side.

"Jester Hornsby the Fifth, who are your people?"

Jester lifted his voice. "The Swartza!" Another thrust.

"Who are your enemies?"

"Those who rebel against us!" The sword was almost completely inside his chest.

"And who is your queen?"

"Lady Seizette!"

Lady Seizette pushed the remainder of the sword hilt dramatically into the teen's chest so that it vanished within him. She stood up triumphantly, her arms in the air as brilliance gleamed off her as if from a mirror ball.

"I, Lady Seizette, still queen of those who pledge to me, grant you, Jester Hornsby the Fifth, a place in my legion. Now rise a Swartza."

She took the keys off his shoulders and Jester Hornsby the Fifth stood up to deafening applause. The diamond keys shrank back down into her hands and she turned toward a servant who approached with a lowered head and a red velvet pillow extended out to her. Lady Seizette took a ring off the velvet and gave it to Jester. Nathanial was too far away to see but he was sure it was the same one as Trid and Captain Malik wore. Jester put the ring on, turned to face the students and pumped his bedecked fist into the air. The cheers doubled in volume.

After dinner, Nathanial walked toward his room, his ears still ringing from all the crazy cheering. What he'd just witnessed unsettled him. He'd read about cults and now he could see why he'd been told these people were like one. Perhaps there weren't goat sacrifices going on (or maybe transmogrification class was close enough), but there was definitely brainwashing. All these kids were essentially being brainwashed to believe the ravings of a self-proclaimed queen. He really needed to get himself and his friends out of there!

He mumbled good night to everyone in the hall and entered his room in a trance. Was he really going to have to go through with taking an oath from that power-hungry woman? Wouldn't that make him a part of her legion? Was it possible to just run away after that?

Looking at the book on his bedside table he wondered if there was anything in it about breaking oaths. He ran over to it and started flipping pages. It was too long! There had to be a table of contents. Nathanial flipped to the opening pages when something caught his attention: a symbol like the Egyptian Eye of Ra with a circular embellishment around it. He'd seen that very same image in his personal journal. He rubbed his finger over the symbol and words formed over it.

State inquiry.

Nathanial licked his lips. "Uh, I'd like to see something on Swartza oaths?" he said. "Like, what happens if you break one?"

Nathanial had to sit back quickly as the pages began to flip of their own accord until there it was: Breaking the Swartza Oath. He couldn't believe it. Nathanial leaned in close to read.

I myself have never dared to ponder on the idea of breaking my oath to the queen, but today I witnessed one who had. It was a young French love sprite who so foolishly fell for the human she was assigned to work on. She wanted to leave our campaign to marry this factory; what a disgrace.

My dear queen, as clever as she is, left the love sprite her free will and did not decline her request. When I asked her why she would release one of her legion she explained how the bond of the oath is a bond to herself, and she would not have someone in her legion who was not committed to her. To break the oath is to break the queen's own heart, and in turn the traitor's heart shall be broken.

It was a quiet sort of vengeance, as my queen did not tell me or even the love sprite what it truly meant to break the oath. Out of curiosity I kept watch on the love sprite to see what this punishment would look like. Within a year she was with child and the man she had left our queen for had been pulled away from her in

greater service to our cause.
I could see it was a curse at
work then. Only heartache and
woe accompanied the sprite.
Every endeavor failed, every
friend was lost and every
dream crushed. She would meet
an early grave and the curse
that was set in blood will pass
into that babe and perhaps
even into generations to come.
A very clever trick indeed.

Nathanial set the book down, disheartened. This sounded an awful lot like the blood curse that had affected Aliya. If Seizette used such curses herself, of course she would know how to stop Aliya's.

After hours of staring up at his canopy he figured there was only one thing for it. He would have to take the oath, free his friends, get to Hyperion, and see if he could learn that diamond-implanting trick Seizette had used to stop Aliya's curse.

Within the week, two more sprites were called

to take the trials. The weekend had come and the latest student still hadn't passed after two days. Nathanial was halfway through the history of the Crossing Treaty and only becoming more convinced that Lady Seizette was mentally imbalanced. He didn't know how anyone could be so deluded. She seriously thought she was a supreme being who could use every other creature on the planet to give her whatever she wanted, and that everyone else saw her the same way. Talk about a god complex. The worst part was that there had been a time when she'd had thousands of people at her beck and call.

Nathanial skipped to the end of the book to gain some clarification on how the Crossing Treaty had actually ended Seizette's reign. It turned out that both sides had had to give a little to get a little. The rebels wanted Seizette to step down and the supporters of the monarchy no longer wanted to negotiate terms with the humans, so they conceded each other's terms to end the bloodshed.

It was time Nathanial took a break from reading, however. It was Sunday, after all.

"Hey, Aliya," Nathanial said when he met up with her in the greenhouse.

"Hey, how's the reading?"

"The usual. Seizette's a psycho."

Aliya laughed. Nathanial felt a little guilty about not giving her any more details, but the whole thing was pretty depressing and he wanted to save her that. He hadn't even told her about finding out what breaking the oath would do. She probably wouldn't allow him to go through with it and they'd be stuck there forever.

"I found the plant that's supposed to cure the hiccups," Aliya said, pointing at a spikey three-leafed bulb. "Too bad we don't have any to test it."

"I can give you the hiccups," Nathanial said excitedly. "Didn't I tell you about that trick? In the book they used it on a factory that was housing the enemy. Shook them all out."

Aliya laughed even harder. "Wow, some of the things these sprites do sound so ridiculous."

"At first it does, but I don't want to tell you what they did next."

Aliya's smile vanished.

"Anyway." Nathanial cleared his throat, and then he noticed Aliya was looking behind him. "What?" Nathanial turned around.

Captain Malik was standing behind him. "Nathanial, it's your time."

"What?" Nathanial gawped. "But that can't be. There's someone still in there."

"He failed." Captain Malik lifted a single

eyebrow. "Follow me."

Nathanial was horrorstruck. Aliya mirrored the expression.

"Good luck," she whispered.

THE DIAMOND TRIALS

The room Nathanial was led into shone like the corona of the sun. It was nothing but jutting, sparkling diamonds that glowed brightly from within. The floor was the only smooth crystal in the room. Nathanial had to be careful making his way to the center of the space. One wrong turn and he could poke an eye out.

"This is where the trials are held," Captain Malik said, coming to a full stop where multiple diamond points converged, leaving only enough space for one person to stand.

"Okaaay," Nathanial said, perplexed.

Captain Malik moved from the spot and Nathanial took his place within the confining points of the diamond.

"Are you sure you want to go through with this?"

This made Nathanial doubly perplexed. Was this concern from his nemesis? "Why? What do you care?"

"Why would I care about a boy attempting to join the ranks of men in the greatest legion on the planet? Or why would I care about a fraud planning to break his oath, thereby ruining his life, which he naively thought he would be bettering by this action?"

Nathanial held his breath. So it wasn't exactly concern being shown here. It was a calling out. "The second one," Nathanial answered and crossed his arms.

Captain Malik bent down close to Nathanial and said, "If you do this, you are one of us or you are nothing. You still don't seem to understand that a contract is binding. You may have squirmed out of one before but only with help from other well-informed sprites. You have barely even begun to become a sprite, and yet you have the audacity to sign up for one of our most exalted trials. You are a fool, and mark my words this will be your last foolish mistake."

Captain Malik turned and left the room.

"Oh man." Nathanial gulped down his rising panic. "What am I doing?"

A figure appeared suddenly in front of him and Nathanial jumped back. It was the ghostly form of Lady Seizette.

"Welcome, potential Swartza. You have decided to take the Diamond Trials; congratulations," the holograph-like Seizette said with a smile.

"What is this? Some kind of a recording?" Nathanial questioned the softness of the voice that didn't have the same sultry quality of the real Seizette.

"I will be explaining the rules to you," she continued, and the diamond room around them transformed into a lofty, fire-lit office with wood paneling. "The diamond holds the history and memories of thousands. Today we will only be exploring a few of the greatest moments among them. You must choose an action when you are instructed to, and if you prove to possess bravery, loyalty, and knowledge, like those who came before you, you will have passed."

"Oh boy," Nathanial said, licking his lips, and looked at the two male sprites frozen in midconversation before him. He wondered if they were holograms like Seizette, and if the diamond was somehow projecting the scene around him. He slowly walked toward the red sprite, a hand out before him in case he was about to run into one of the sharp diamonds that had been surrounding him moments before. He made it to the stranger and touched his deep red cheek.

"Not a hologram," he voiced his thoughts. "The diamond holds memories; this is probably all in my head. Maybe I only think I can feel this because my brain tells me I do." He poked the cheek a few more times. "Seems so real."

"Ability enhancers are not permitted during the trials."

"What?" Nathanial said, turning horrified to the ghostly Seizette. She reached toward his chest. "No!" he cried and tried to protect his necklace, but somehow the ghostly hand was able to pass through his cupped hands and shirt, grab hold of the necklace, and break it off his neck.

"Good luck," the recording said, with a sickening smile as she held firm to the necklace and disappeared.

Game over. What was he going to do now? Nathanial had never performed a trick without the necklace. He was going to fail and be stuck in the trials forever.

"No, I don't care what the sprites of Cantabury are whining about now. Just give them an extra column of honey this quarter and tell them to shut it," said the red sprite in a British accent, as he passed Nathanial and went around the room setting fire to the tips of iron sconces with the touch of his palm. He wore old-fashioned attire: gold button-up clasps on an eggshell vest with a puffy maroon undershirt and tight cotton pants. His boat-shaped hat was adorned with grass twigs and a grape centerpiece.

Sprites of Cantabury, Nathanial thought. Weren't they the ones to start the riots of the third rebellion in the Crossing Treaty book?

"I would, sir, but you don't understand: it's not just the sprites of Cantabury any longer," said an alabaster sprite with a slight country drawl. He looked an awful lot like the sketch of Trid's grandfather, only some years younger, as his cactus-tipped mustache wasn't too impressive yet. "Their dispute has spread to the neighboring town. The workers on Factory Bronson are asking questions now. They say that they have negotiated the best deal with their factory in all the kingdoms. That the only way the salt quantities coming out of the Swartza factories can beat their own is if factory abuse is taking place there."

"Ugh, bug-wallop," cursed the red sprite. "What would you have me do, then?"

For a moment Nathanial did not realize the red sprite had turned to him while asking the question. When he did realize it, the shock of it kept him quiet.

"Well?" The alabaster sprite turned to Nathanial too. "What do you suppose my answer was when the general asked me what I'd have him do?"

"Oh." Nathanial's voice broke. "What did you

say?" So he should have studied the history first and not so much the tricks, darn it. After racking his brain he said, "You suggest replacing all the factory workers with loyalists. The general decides that you, Captain Whirlvauhl Brunt, will be transferred to the council of Lady…ugh, Queen Seizette, to present her with this idea, as it is beyond his power to enforce. You inform her of the situation and she agrees to your proposal."

The two sprites smiled and the room faded to black. Nathanial opened his eyes and saw he was still in the diamond room. It confirmed for him that it must have all been in his mind. The translucent Lady Seizette stood in front of him.

"Correct." Seizette smiled. "That was a trial in knowledge. Now for a trial in bravery."

The room shifted again but this time so too did Nathanial's clothing. It was such a strange sensation, trying to hold on to any sense of reality. He was in full knight-of-the-round-table-style armor, the Swartza keys crossing a sword stamped to his chest, a helmet with an eye-slit on his head, and a long sword in his hand. He had to catch his step as the sudden weight of the armor threw him off-balance and he was pushed onward by a trooper behind him until he caught up with the one just ahead. They had a sneaky demeanor, all jogging quietly in a half-crouched position. They were moving in a line inside a fallen log that towered two stories high and had patches of rot allowing Nathanial to occasionally spot the bodies colliding in battle on the other side.

"We have orders to wait here," whispered the leader of the troop as he came to a halt next to a large gap in the fallen tree. The half a dozen men grouped up around their leader.

Nathanial looked beyond and noticed the fighting had stopped. Everyone's attention was on a small hill. Nathanial moved past the tree opening to get a better look. There was something very familiar about this whole scene. Queen Seizette was high above the battlefield, her gown catching the only light on that dark bloody stage. Her hair was twisted high atop her head, providing ample real estate for the towering spikes of her diamond crown. A golden-armored figure was walking up the hill toward the queen but he addressed the crowd as he climbed.

"Too much sprite blood has been spilled over this folly. What will it take to make you all see there is no reason for hate between us?" the figure implored the hundred fatigued sprites before him.

"You." Nathanial felt a tug on his arm and looked around to see the leader beckoning him.

"Come with me."

Nathanial followed him through shrubbery that cut along the edge of the field and ended halfway up the hill only a few yards away from where the golden-armored sprite was standing. He was coming to the end of his speech. Nathanial knew this because he had heard the speech before.

"So for the sake of that future, I ask you now, is it not time we put down our swords and find a compromise. Or are you willing to pass your weapons on to your children when you fall?"

If this was indeed the speech Nathanial remembered from a reenactment where Spassel had played the role of this beseeching knight in gold, then this was the part where he was about to die.

"Now!" As the leader of his troop pushed Nathanial out into the open, several other sprites who had been waiting in ambush came from the opposite side; while at the same time, from behind Seizette, came the ear-splitting roar of a bear. Nathanial's entire attention fell on the giant beast, whose leathery wings put the world into shadow. General Grantz had come to put this dispute to an end.

"Watch out," warned the Swartza leader, and he pointed to the unexpected sight of the golden knight being forced right into Nathanial's path.

The sword was coming down on him. He had just enough time to block the knight's sword with his own blade, and then he was embroiled in combat. He was blocking and fainting, dodging and parrying. Strangely, this too felt familiar. The strokes were almost like a training session with Boss and that gave him an idea. Nathanial lunged, twisted, and swiveled his weapon along the golden knight's blade so that he was able to lift his sword and watch his opponent's fly in an arc across the field.

There was a moment of triumph: the move Boss had used on him in their final session had worked on this great warrior…and then there was the gut-plummeting realization of what he'd done. The hero was disarmed, and was quickly swallowed up by the Swartza army.

The field vanished into darkness and Nathanial opened his eyes once again to the room of diamonds. He was panting and still held his hand aloft as if he had a sword.

"Congratulations," said the ghostly Seizette. "You have proved your bravery. Now let's see where your loyalties lie. You will be requested to perform the appropriate trick affiliated with the given task."

Nathanial felt disoriented from the boomerang

of tasks and repeated the words "perform the appropriate trick," in hopes of grounding himself for a moment. He rubbed the spot where his necklace should have been, and felt sick. It truly wasn't there. He'd half hoped it'd just been a trick in the memory.

The room swirled and changed again. He now sat beside Queen Seizette in what looked like the interior of a horse-drawn coach. She was more beautiful than ever in her full queen's attire that included a delicate diamond crown. Her hair was let loose now and curtained her pale face.

There were sounds of fighting: swords clanging, sprites screaming, the world crashing right outside the coach doors; but you wouldn't have thought so from the calm look Queen Seizette displayed. She stood up and opened the door of the coach, taking a few steps out onto royal purple carpet flanked by armored guards. Nathanial followed and found they were standing upon a giant centipede's back. Behind Seizette's sitting carriage were many elegantly carved compartmentalized cars, surely filled with the comforts any queen should travel with, may she be dining, dressing, or dreaming of world domination.

Nathanial was surprised that there was not a full-on war, going by the racket he had heard, but there seemed to at least be a skirmish. The queen's tail of escorts was being attacked by a swift, fully armored, double-sword-wielding sprite, who had just struck down two guards with a single thrust, jumped over an attacker from the side, and was now flying toward an oncoming battalion. Nathanial thought this gold-plated knight looked like the same man he had just disarmed in the last battle, but that sprite was supposed to have been killed. Had this event taken place before that or was he missing something?

The queen stood there and allowed twenty more of her men to be struck down before she finally said, "Enough." At the flick of her wrist the guards backed off and the warrior approached.

"The mighty Conrad Baldric," Queen Seizette said without needing to see the sprite's face behind his visor. "Voice of the people, savior of the disgraced, bringer of the light, all that tosh and nonsense. How many times have you come for me now? I've lost count. Don't you know everyone thinks you're dead from our last encounter on Mount Lassen? I suppose you thought it a good idea to keep it that way. Maybe you hoped I'd forgotten about you. Tell me, why do you fight for the pathetic dregs of society when you could be a king by my side?"

Conrad removed his helmet and Nathanial gasped. It was Boss, a golden god version of him, but undoubtedly him. His thick flames of hair fell sweaty around his strong brow. Had Nathanial really just fought Boss on Mount Lassen?

"I don't fight for power," Conrad said imploringly. "I fight so that we can live equally and without the need to abuse our gifts. We have the ability to bring out the best in nature, but you only seem to want to bend it to your will. We can make things grow where there was wasteland, bring life where there was death. How can a species with this talent turn its efforts to chaos? Why would you want to make slaves of your own kind as well as the humans when we could all join together for a better world? Branding them as factories rather than allies, and using them unlawfully without their knowledge, is that not beneath you? Will you not be happy until you've downgraded us all into your service?"

The queen wore a small smile all through Conrad's speech, and it did not falter afterward. She took a step closer to him and said, "You have just slaughtered half of my escort in front of me and you speak of life where there was death. You are no more than a hypocrite and you must pay for your arrogance."

"You could have called them off at any time.

You enjoyed watching them put their lives at risk for you. And if you look closer, like you never do, you'd see your men are only wounded."

"If you truly wanted to save lives you would cease your resistance. I have implored you to join me before. I am not in the habit of asking twice." The queen turned to Nathanial and said, to his horror, "Punish him."

Nathanial felt the blood drain from his head. He recalled the details of performing the trick that was used on Boss from the book. It was a degrading trick that he did not want to do. Even if it was all just a test, a sick, twisted test that wasn't real, he did not want to see Boss punished before his eyes, and absolutely not by his own hand. Whether he could do it without the necklace was no longer the point; he just wouldn't.

"I won't," Nathanial muttered.

"Punish him," the queen ordered again. "Prove your loyalty."

Nathanial knew it was a simulation. He knew he wouldn't really be punishing Boss, it wasn't real, but the trick he would be performing would be real, and it was one that should never be used. A nameless curse, Phlegm had called it. It was the reason Boss could never open up to Nathanial, the reason he was so secretive. He continued to shake his head as he refused to convince himself it was okay to try it. His other choice was to be stuck there forever….No, he'd figure another way out. Nathanial backed away.

The queen advanced on him and grabbed his shoulder. Pain immediately grasped his entire body, a shocking, electrocuting pain. "If you do not perform the appropriate trick then the trick shall be performed on you."

Shame. Sick, twisted shame writhed through the core of Nathanial's being. He was a horrible person. How could he have disappointed his queen this way? He was the scum of the earth who didn't deserve to breathe the same air as this beautiful queen. He deserved punishment.

Nathanial writhed on the ground, kicking. He began pulling his own hair and slapping his face, screaming out his sorrow. How could he even have conceived of betraying Seizette? She was a perfect being who deserved worship and he was going to break his oath to her. What was wrong with him?

Nathanial was staring up at the angry Queen Seizette in complete despair when a second, composed version of her stepped through the first, dissipating the vision into mist. Business-attired Seizette bent down to Nathanial with a pitying smile.

"Oh, Nathanial," she said to his crumpled form. "What were you thinking, child? Captain Malik baited you into this, you realize. He told you Sidian wouldn't come to you otherwise, didn't he? I don't think he likes you very much. Promoting him from mere tracker to full-honored captain for tempting you to the school was not enough for him. He wanted to prove to me that you do not belong here."

Seizette put her hand on Nathanial's forehead and the shame softened into vague disappointment.

"I'm sorry," Nathanial moaned.

"I know, sweetheart," she said, and pushed his sweaty hair out of his face. "Unfortunately, you did display a rebellious nature that I can't ignore. If only you had let yourself complete your schooling here, you would have come to see the truth: that the Swartza are at the apex of nature and we belong on top. I didn't want to condition you this way, but…" She stood up and dusted off her hands. "Even the general needed some time in the diamond before he was ready for war."

As Seizette walked away the memory images of Boss and Queen Seizette faded into a white cloud that swallowed Nathanial.

He felt nausea rising up in him. He curled up into a ball and yelled, "No, please, come back. I'm sorry. My queen, forgive me. Come back."

He lay there for a time; he didn't care how long, until, "Nathanial!" A voice was calling to him from far away but he didn't want to hear it. It was not his queen's voice; he did not care for any other voice. "Nathanial, get up." But he would not. His place was on the floor, beneath the feet of his queen. "Nathanial!" A jolt shocked Nathanial's eyes open. "I'm sorry, I had to, are you okay?"

It was the disembodied voice, but no longer disembodied. Nathanial looked up through bloodshot eyes and saw a face he hadn't seen in over a year. It was the pretty, petite, golden-haired sprite who had helped him through his ten-year wish hearing. Her eyes sparkled crystal blue concern into his.

"Gem?" Nathanial asked, wondering if she was real. "Are you a part of my punishment? Shock me again. I deserve it."

"What? No, I'm in the diamond, remember, and now so are you. I've opened up a safe space around us so we can talk."

"What?" Nathanial got to his knees and looked around. The small room around them glistened like uncut diamond. The walls were claustrophobically close. "What do you mean?"

"You failed the trials. Everyone gets put into the diamond when they fail the trials."

"I deserve to be here. I'm a horrible person. I failed. Let Seizette get what she can from me in here." Nathanial collapsed back onto the floor and began pulling his hair again.

"Oh, maybe you do need another jolt." And Gem put her hand to his forehead with a ZAP.

"Ouch!" Nathanial screamed and sat back up.

"Better?"

Nathanial sat there wide-eyed for a moment then said, "Better. Sorry. Don't know what I was thinking. Right, how do we get out of here?"

"I don't know. You were my only contact on the outside."

"Contact...We could contact Aliya." And with those words something strange happened. Hundreds of memories, Aliya's memories, flooded into Nathanial's mind. She had been raised in Israel, her mother had been killed in the war, her sister was about to join the army; and there was the face of her Mataunte, telling her a curse was to blame for all these tragedies.

Suddenly, as if triggered by the thought of the curse, a soft voice said, "A blood curse can only be drawn out by the one who put it there." It was the wish sprite from Aliya's hearing, and with those words it was as if time began to rewind. It went so far back that Aliya could not have been the one to witness these events.

The Mataunte who had helped raise Aliya stood focused in the center of the swirling vision. Her face lost all its wrinkles and became youthful as time rewound. When all came to a stop she stood as a young and beautiful sprite the color of a pink rose, pleading with another sprite who was a few years her junior and shared her pouty lips and luscious ripples of cotton-candy hair.

"You cannot do this, Jessabelle," Mataunte beseeched. She was speaking French, but somehow Nathanial understood. "You know the queen's plans for him. She put you on him to seduce him to her cause. She will not let you two leave together. To watch one of her own choose a human way of life over all that she has been crusading for! Do you really think that is not the greatest offense you could give her?"

"You do not know the queen as I do, sissy. She is more compassionate than you give her credit for. She has already allowed me release from the oath."

Mataunte gasped. "No, Jessabelle, you didn't." She looked on the verge of tears. "There is no release from that oath, you know this. She will seek vengeance on you. She lets no one go without punishment. What have you done?"

The memory shifted to another stage but the players remained the same. A crying newborn baby screamed in the arms of an older Mataunte, and a still-young Jessabelle lay at their side in a small bed, looking weak.

"This is her doing." Mataunte spoke angrily at the sight of her dying sister. "First she keeps you locked away in that diamond until after the war, just in case she has a use for you, and now she releases you only to suffer this fatal blood curse. You know now this babe will suffer the same fate."

"No!" Jessabelle's tears ran down her cheeks as she rubbed the baby's hand between her fingers. "Teach her of the wish sprites. Tell her of the ten-year wish. It is strong. It can beat this. I love you, Aliya." She kissed her fingertips and placed them on baby Aliya's cheek. "She looks so much like her father," she said with a small smile and played with the round tips of the baby's ears. Then she groaned, turned away, and closed her eyes forever.

Night cascaded around Nathanial and he saw Mataunte standing in front of a house with Aliya still bundled in her arms. Mataunte closed her eyes in concentration. A few more wrinkles appeared on her face and the pink of her skin faded into tan. The color of her hair salted into strings of gray and the tips of her ears shrank down. She knocked on the door and a man answered.

"Hello," Mataunte said with a French accent entangled within rough Hebrew words. "I understand that you have lost your wife to war and just recently a baby girl to illness. You now find yourself alone with a young daughter to raise and support. I would like to offer you my services in child-rearing if you would be so kind as to allow me to bring in this child to be loved as if she were your own."

Nathanial was not sure if Mataunte was using her tricks as a love sprite to reach out to the man or if it was his own humanity that kindled his heart, but he moved the cloth away from Aliya's face and stared down at the innocent baby for quite a while before opening his arms in a gesture for Mataunte to enter the house.

Nathanial knew the rest of this story. Mataunte did teach the ten-year wish to Aliya and it became her only hope of saving herself and her sister. But now Nathanial knew why the wish sprite had said the curse did not affect her sister.

Aliya had grown up assuming her mother was the same woman her father told her stories about. The one who went to war and never came back. Aliya blamed the blood curse and feared it would use the army to take her sister and then herself when the time came. Though Mataunte knew Aliya was the only one truly at risk, she let the girl's fears drive each wish so that it might one day break the curse.

But failure was a part of the curse, and although the wish was granted it had the consequence of trapping Aliya aboard the pirate ship Argosy. Yet, Nathanial thought, in spite of the odds that had been stacked against her, she had found him, and in the end he was the reason why Aliya had been brought to the very person who had cursed her bloodline. Only Seizette could have put a stop to the blood curse, and that was exactly what she'd done. Maybe, just maybe, even with the worst curse imaginable set upon you, real determination to overcome it could win the day. Well, determination and a little blind luck, he supposed.

Nathanial fell out of the memories and found himself back on the diamond floor. "Whoa, what was that?" He put a hand to his head.

"You just accessed a set of memories through the diamond," Gem said, helping Nathanial to his feet.

"Yeah, Aliya's, but it was more than that. I could see things I don't think she knows about."

"She must have been in the diamond. It can read blood memory and will connect Aliya's memories with the memories of any blood relation that have also been uploaded. It's strange that you were able to access them, you not being a crystal sprite, but on the other hand you aren't any specific breed; you haven't chosen your color. I think that might be giving you an advantage."

"That would explain a lot, and Aliya was in the diamond, and it seems like her mother was too." Nathanial blinked several times. "I was just thinking about Aliya because…because she could get us out. I told her about you. We had a plan to get the key. She should be able to find Seizette's office. How did you talk to me from in here before? Can we find her? What about Spassel? Where is he?"

Gem was amazingly patient given all the questions and the state of confusion Nathanial seemed to be experiencing. She answered about Spassel first. "I'm the only one who can visit others in here because of my old blood trait as a crystal grower. I have spoken to Spassel and told him to be ready, that I'll come to get him when you give me the key. I will have to contact Aliya alone. I am sorry, Nathanial, but when I leave, you will lose all sense of time and reality once again. I am the only thing keeping this diamond room from closing in on you."

Nathanial nodded. He had a feeling he was about to experience first-hand what Aliya had gone through for so many years of her life, a sense of timelessness. He watched Gem walk into a diamond wall and vanish. He wondered how old Aliya would be the next time he saw her.

RECONDITIONING

Nathanial sat utterly exhausted on the diamond floor. After Gem had left, a white fog steadily built around him until it was a complete whiteout. Seizette's trick had been zapped away by Gem, probably because it was only the memory of a trick, but his current depression arose from his failure. Sidian would not accept his commands. Even if Aliya did get the key, and he was pulled from the diamond, how would they escape without him having taken the oath? Or what if she couldn't get to the key at all? How long would he be stuck there? Centuries perhaps. His poor mother would be devastated.

The opaque fog felt as though it was solidifying around him. Panic creeped in as his body constricted within the diamond until the fog seemed to seep into Nathanial's own mind; all thoughts ceased.

It was worse than darkness. It was nothingness. There was a buzzing in his ears and the thudding of his heartbeat drummed in the recesses of the deafening silence. Time truly did not exist, only an agonizing present that could not change. He felt he was waiting for a dreadful event to start but did not know what it was, or when it would start, or why he was waiting, only that he wanted it to be over but felt it never would be.

Then, after what felt like a lifetime of sitting, waiting, dreading, but not thinking, the strangest thing happened: his old human room that he'd called the Cube of Solitude appeared around him. The Jupiter poster taunted him from his ceiling, reminding him that the only exploring he'd ever do would be in dreams, and his wall of books would be his only company.

His thoughts drifted in aimless confusion for a moment and then he coughed. Another one of his fits was coming on. He could feel the tickle in his throat intensifying and his eyes watering. He rushed to his bathroom sink and ran the hot water before pulling some rags from a drawer. After a deep breath, he released a volley of coughs.

He struggled to run the rags under the warm water, barely managing it. Fighting to reach his bed, he collapsed into his covers and placed the warm rags over his coughing face, trying to sooth his throat with their humidity. He didn't know how long he lay there convulsing but when the voice called to him it seemed to come from miles away.

Nathanial sat up. "Mom," he called between coughs.

His door slowly swung open. This was both frightening and exciting. He hated being trapped in his room but he also knew it was the only thing keeping him alive.

It wasn't like his mother to open the door. Her blurry outline began to solidify as it approached his bed. Her sweet crimson smile brought him comfort.

"Mom, it's you, isn't it? I've missed you so much." Nathanial let the soft hand brush his sweaty hair off his brow.

"Yes, dear. I will take care of you now. Don't you fret," Seizette said and pulled Nathanial down into her lap.

For a moment Nathanial knew it was not his mom, but as the soreness in his throat began to fade, his breathing normalized, and the sound of her humming voice lifted his heart, he felt a motherly love that had the power to heal him, and he lay there, content.

"Nathanial!" three voices screamed so loudly they could have burst an eardrum.

Nathanial opened his eyes to the small diamond

room; the visions of his bedroom and Seizette clinging on like a vivid dream. The fog had cleared and he stared at the three figures before him, feeling he had been wrenched from happiness. They looked at him expectantly, like he should know them, and he tried to recall.

"How long has it been?" he asked, his memory returning.

Mila laughed, her proud punk-rock stance matching her permanent confidence. She shook back her razor-cut curtains of black hair and said, "Not more than a few minutes, from what Gem tells us. Always the one for dramatics, aren't you, Nat?"

Nathanial furrowed his eyebrows. "Then how'd you get here, Mila?" He wouldn't have been surprised to see just Gem and Aliya, but Mila should have been back at Hyperion by now.

"Nice to see you too," she said. "I've been trying to rescue your stupid head ever since you ran off. Then Spaz thought he'd play the hero, waltzed right up to his uncle in the kitchen to ask for help, and got himself crystalized for it. I could say the same thing about you, though, trying to play the hero, thinking you'd take the oath! Do you know what breaking that deal would have gotten you?"

"It is nice to see you, Mila," Nathanial said,

getting to his feet. Mila always did enjoy scolding him, but he usually deserved it, and his warm smile toward her said so. She smirked back at him and the maroon tinge in her lips offset the violet sparkles in her eyes.

"I'll go get Spassel," Gem said. Aliya handed a diamond-bedazzled glove to Gem, "I'll be quick. The space will hold its form until I get back." And she passed into a wall.

"I was relieved to have Mila's help," Aliya said, her posture tense. "She came to me just after you were taken for the trials and we searched for the key in Seizette's office together, it's that diamond glove I just gave Gem. She told us how to use it to get through the diamond walls in Seizette's office; that's how we are in here with you now. Nathan, Mila told me what would have happened if you succeeded in the trials and if we went through with breaking the oath. You would have been stricken with the blood curse. I am so sorry. I didn't know. I never should have suggested you do this."

Nathanial had known the consequences of breaking the oath and he felt bad that he'd kept it a secret from her. He always seemed to find himself doing that, even though she was the person he most wanted to be open with. Now he knew the truth of her past and had no clue how to share it with her.

"It's okay, Aliya," he said heavily. "It was my choice to try this, but also probably for the best that I failed miserably." He smiled at her.

She laughed, a sound that was almost a cry.

"And it looks like I have some pretty awesome friends to come save me from myself," he added, thankful to have them both standing there before him.

Gem came back into the room. "I can't find Spassel," she said.

OH CHUTE

"**W**hat?" the three sprites Gem was facing chorused in panic.

"I spoke to him just days ago," Gem said. "I think the trials have caused a shift in the diamond. Room is being made for the new failed students and absorbed memories."

"Is there anything we can do?" Nathanial asked desperately.

"I do have an idea," Gem said. "Nathanial, I can take you deeper into the diamond along with me now that I have the key." She held up her hand that wore the sparkling glove. "We can use your connection to Spassel and your…talent, perhaps, to find him."

Mila and Aliya each took turns locking a quizzical gaze with Nathanial, clearly asking what talent Gem was talking about. He knew she meant his ability to access the diamond memories without being a crystal sprite and feared Mila was trying to read his mind. Thankfully, Nathanial had learned how to stop her a while back from succeeding in that venture. He did not want her to know Aliya's secret before she herself did.

"We have to be quick." Gem added. "I don't want to leave Aliya and Mila alone in the diamond for too long or the walls will close in on them, and I don't think it's safe to take them out of the diamond while we look for Spassel."

"I'm willing to try whatever you think is best," Nathanial said with determination, and walked toward the hand that Gem stretched out to him. He let himself be guided into the crystal as Gem pushed through with the glinting gloved hand she held out before them.

It was like jumping into a pool and being told it was all right to breathe. He held on to his last breath until his burning lungs forced his mouth to open. The large inhale sounded muffled and so too did Gem's voice as she tried to calm him.

"Just breathe, Nathanial," she said, keeping a tight hold of his hand. "It's okay, I've got you."

Nathanial kept his eyes on hers for several more determined inhales, letting each of his breaths be conducted by the rise and fall of her hand, until his panic waned.

"I'm okay," Nathanial finally said. His voice sounded as if he was hearing it through ears clogged with wax.

"I need you to remember Spassel. Think of the first time you met him," Gem said with an encouraging nod. "I'm connected with you through the diamond key so the memory should be visible to both of us and hopefully take us physically closer to Spassel if this goes right."

Nathanial remembered the first time he met Spassel and smiled.

Within the thick diamond next to him, Nathanial saw the small, wide-eyed, white-haired sprite boy wearing the Hyperion school uniform, but there was a milky texture to him so that Nathanial knew Spassel was not truly there. The little sprite muttered in agitation, "You're not dressed. We'll be late!"

"That's it," Gem said, also looking at the image of Spassel. Then the thick, semi-solid walls shifted into motion blur before suddenly stopping again.

A memory projected above them. He knew it was Spassel's from a story he had shared with Nathanial at Hyperion. A Chihuahua the size of a smart car was licking a toddler-sized Spassel almost to death. A yellow mom and dad, very panicked, were trying to pull their son away from the persistent and suffocating licks.

"You've got his memory link; now try to think of something defining about him. Something that can pull us further toward him," Gem said.

Another memory streamed up into the crystal above them, this one he and Spassel shared. Nathanial watched himself and Spassel standing in the wooden halls of the great tree Hyperion. Nathanial remembered how worried he had been that he might be acting too human and hadn't been sure how Spassel would react if he found out the truth of his origins.

"You don't have the natural reservations most of us do," Spassel was saying. "You should know why I'm embarrassed. First because I told you my parents are yellow and now because you caught me playing one of the bravest heroes of all time when clearly that role should be portrayed by an orange sprite. You've probably even figured out what I see my inner calling as and have no protest against that either."

"Mmm..." the projection of Nathanial pursed his lips and nodded. Spassel examined his face.

"Head council member," Spassel finally admitted. "I think it's my best shot at making a real difference."

Then, behind Gem, was a projection seen

through Spassel's point of view, of Nathanial running from the century kids before streaking into a blur. Nathanial felt a twist of anger toward those kids. They'd hated him for being a human turned sprite.

"We're getting closer," Gem said.

The next memory domed up and around the pair like a 360-degree movie projector casting images onto the glass of their snow globe–like surroundings. Mila and Spassel's milky forms stood in a wooded nightscape.

Mila was looking at Spassel with a very serious expression, saying, "What are you doing here? You shouldn't be here, Spaz!"

"Oh, so you think you're the only one who cares about Nat, do you?" Spassel said, hands on hips. "I heard those skunk-tail century thugs complaining about Nat being accepted into Swartza High. I mean, it was kind of funny to see them so upset after all they tried to do to get him in trouble with the Swartza, but I just couldn't believe Nat would willingly want to go to that school. He was having so much fun at Hyperion."

"Was he now," Mila said, with a crooked smile.

"Yes!" Spassel insisted. "We were fast friends. I can't leave him in the hands of the corrupt!"

"And what's your plan?"

"I have a plan," Spassel stated confidently. "What about you? I heard Boss and the others telling you to go back to Hyperion."

"You were spying." Mila shot a glare like daggers out of her eyes.

"I'm not a spy." Spassel took offense. "I just happened to be going by your camp on my way to execute my most amazing plan when I happened to overhear. Now, do you want to stop badgering me and team up, or are you going to go back to Hyperion like you were told?"

Mila looked a little proud of Spassel then; and that's when the world spun.

Nathanial grasped tighter to Gem's hand as the disorientation almost threw him off balance. The diamond that encompassed them now appeared to glow with early morning light and Nathanial recognized the exterior gothic walls of Swartza High.

Spassel and Mila waited behind a statue for a Swartza guard to turn the corner of the school before dashing for a door. Behind it were loud chopping and grinding sounds. The duo snuck through the door and followed the noises into a massive kitchen.

Nathanial bent his knees to solidify his stance as the moving walls once again threatened his balance as the memory followed Mila and Spassel's journey.

"That's my uncle over there," Spassel said, pointing to a yellow sprite in a floppy white hat and apron, who was reaching up to break the tip off a stalactite-sized carrot.

"This was your big plan." Mila scoffed. "Talk to your uncle. Spassel, we are in the lion's den here. Any one of these sprites could turn you in."

"No, my uncle says everyone here despises their work. Trust me." Spassel, self-assured, walked boldly out toward his uncle.

Mila tried to reach for him, but when she saw more cooks entering the room she disappeared back into the shadows.

Within a minute guards had surrounded Spassel and were pulling him out of the grasp of his terrified uncle.

"This is it," Gem said, looking fiercely around. "We've almost found him."

Spassel's petrified stare was gargantuan in the thick air around them. His voice reverberated within the walls. "I'm not a spy." Diamonds crystalized out of his skin. The scream was loud, then muffled, and then silent.

It was as if a bubble had popped. Nathanial could breathe normally. The memory projections on the walls were gone and they stood in a small open space within the diamond. Gem let go of his hand.

There was a small whimper from behind Nathanial and he turned around.

"Spassel!" Nathanial ran to his crumpled form where it lay on the diamond ground. "You okay?"

Spassel turned his pale, wet face slowly toward Nathanial. "Nat, is that you?"

"Yes." Nathanial couldn't help laughing. It was a good sign that Spassel remembered him on sight, and it was so great to see him.

"How you doing, buddy?" Nathanial asked.

"I don't know," Spassel said. "I think I'm okay. I can't remember how I got here. Where is here?"

"Uh." Nathanial looked back at Gem, trying to find the words. "We're in kind of like a diamond prison, I guess. You tried to save me from Swartza High, remember?"

"Oh yeah," Spassel said slowly. "Was that here? I thought I was somewhere else. Gem said something about you looking for a key, but that seemed so long ago."

Gem came over and together she and Nathanial helped Spassel to his feet. "The diamond reconditioning often puts people in a place that's familiar to them," she explained, "but Seizette manipulates the experience to make the captive sympathetic or even grateful to her as she plays a role of providing relief from the very pain she is inflicting. She was supposed to have released all her prisoners of war from these traps after she signed the Crossing Treaty and never use this special trick of hers again."

"I don't think she much cares for other people's rules," Nathanial said. "She's a marches-to-her-own-drum kind of psychopath."

Gem nodded in agreement, then took Nathanial's hand again. "Take Spassel's hand," she said to him. "Just one more big push after this and we are out of here."

This time Nathanial was more prepared for the swim-like walk through the diamond, and he concentrated his efforts on helping Spassel breathe as they quickly waded through the dense atmosphere and back out into the gap where Mila and Aliya stood.

"Spaz!" Mila ran to her little friend and gave him a big hug. "Never, ever again, do you hear me? I make the plans from now on."

Spassel half smiled and said, "Don't blame the plan. Blame my clumsy execution."

Aliya went up to Spassel and held out her hand. "Hi, I'm Aliya. It was very brave of you to come after Nathan." Spassel took her hand and shook it with a blush.

"Aww, he would have done the same for me," Spassel said sweetly.

Nathanial was getting excited to see all his friends together and since Mila seemed to be the plan girl at the moment he looked to her to ask, "What is the current plan, Mila? I can't call Sidian to fly us out of here. Did you bring Ori?"

"Ori couldn't carry us all on her back, but that doesn't matter anyway. She'd be spotted and shot down in a second. Boss was trying to negotiate for your release but even before I left him it was becoming all too clear that Seizette has Swartza in every corner of every establishment and she didn't want to give either of you up. She can do whatever she likes and make it look legal. This entire ordeal with you has really ruffled some feathers, Nat. It's bringing old memories back to life. People remember what a bully Seizette was as queen and they're worried she's gaining that power again. Locking Gem away for granting you your exchange has woken her old enemies up to the danger.

"But, look, we can worry about that later. For now we need to head back to the kitchens. The guards have been doubled around this place, which is no surprise after you were caught, Spaz, but I did get a quiet word with your uncle. He has another way for us to get out."

"Do you know how to get there?" Aliya asked Mila. "This school is a labyrinth.'

"More or less. Gem, can you get us out of this diamond on the first floor?"

Gem nodded and said, "Everyone hold hands and don't let go until we're out." As Nathanial was still closest to her she grabbed his hand again; he took Aliya's, who took Mila's, who grabbed tight to Spassel's and gave it an encouraging shake.

Gem lifted her hand in its diamond-encrusted glove key and pushed through the smooth crystal wall. Perhaps the added bodies made the difference because this time it felt to Nathanial as if they were walking through hurricane-force winds. Not only was breathing difficult but just putting one foot in front of the other was a laborious task. A minute enduring this pressure was sixty seconds too long, but thankfully that's all it was before one by one they came crashing out into a hallway, all stumbling from the sudden lack of resistance.

"I've only seen the school from where the diamonds grow, and this vein is the one from which I've seen food passing by. The kitchen must be close but at least a few corridors away still," Gem said, panting from the expended effort. "We need to be careful not to be seen."

Nathanial followed close behind Mila and Gem with Spassel and Aliya on each side. As they came to the end of the first corridor, Mila and Gem stopped to whisper.

"Which way?" Nathanial asked impatiently, uncomfortable as they stood at the center of a three-way junction.

"Well, well, well, what do we have here?" said a sneering voice. A sprite waltzed into view from a doorway a few yards to their left.

Nathanial cringed. Of all teachers, it had to have been the one who hated him most.

"Aren't you supposed to be in the trials right about now?" Mr. Hutchince asked, ignoring the others and fixating on him.

"I passed," Nathanial said with a small smile.

"Yaaay."

"Sure you did." Mr. Hutchince winked. "And you happen to be near the kitchen because the ordeal left you parched, I'm sure. It has nothing to do with the spy standing beside you, who just happened to be found in that very same place."

Spassel gulped and Nathanial narrowed his eyes. He lost any hope of fooling the spiteful teacher, and anger kindled inside him instead. He was tired of being toyed with. "Look, if you're going to turn us in, just do it. I'm sure your beloved Seizette will reward you for your undying loyalty. Maybe she'll even give you your heart back."

Mr. Hutchince dropped his sneer. Nathanial hadn't wholly understood the advice Trid had given him on how to stop the man, and the curiosity blurted out of him.

"What exactly did she do to you, anyway?" Nathanial asked, standing up straight as the others took a small step back, Aliya keeping a hand on the back of Nathanial's shirt. "I mean, I can almost believe she literally took your heart, with the way you abuse your role as a teacher. You think it's funny to play tricks on your students, do you? Your heart is cold, at the least."

Mr. Hutchince took a single step forward. As

if it was a coordinated dance step, the group took one back, Aliya pulling Nathanial.

"I could have been great," Mr. Hutchince said in a heated whisper. "We all could have been great. As headmaster I would not have made this a lockdown school. I would not teach only the century families. All sprites could learn here."

Nathanial's anger faltered. That almost sounded…not evil.

"I tried to warn the queen that this way is not sustainable," Mr. Hutchince continued as if lost in a memory. "The war was proof, but she would not listen. If she would let me lead this school I could lay the world at her feet, but she would rather cripple my talents, take away my ability to recruit sprites of all color, and lay me low as just another stepping-stone instead of an equal."

Okay, still evil, Nathanial decided.

Mr. Hutchince sighed and his eyes focused on Nathanial again. "One day she will regret the restraints she has put on my heart. She will wish she had let me win her the admiration she deserves instead of trying to do it all herself." His arm lifted slowly until it stopped with a pointed finger indicating a direction. "Go," he said darkly.

"What?" Nathanial gaped. He was lingering in

disbelief when he felt hands pulling on his shirt.

They ran to the large silver doors at the end of the hall. These they quietly peeked through, seeing a hustle and bustle of long white aprons and tall fluffy hats worn by the dozen or so yellow sprites.

Nathanial gazed skyward at the giant fruits and vegetables moving along conveyer belts. They ran through huge chopping machines before splashing down into tanks with dispenser spouts at the base.

The group tiptoed behind boulder-sized apples.

"Your uncle said he was going to request sanitation duty until we meet up with him," Mila said to Spassel. "Fewer sprites in that area of the kitchen." She pointed to a ground-level conveyer belt where sprites were throwing food refuse. It trained along the wall until it passed through a square opening that was labeled Sani-Sort. Next to it was a door with the same sign.

They snuck behind the cover of free-standing shelves packed with food, until they quietly passed through the swinging door.

In the corner of the small noisy space was a slightly rounded sprite with a hay-colored caterpillar mustache, who was occasionally grabbing, with rubber-gloved hands, a piece of food that was heading toward the Dreg Chute, and throwing it into the Goop Chute, or vice versa. Each chute was a square void in the wall, and these were clearly where the loud mechanical sounds, like a sink's garbage disposal, were coming from.

"Uncle Watt," Spassel said softly.

The old yellow sprite turned around, wide-eyed, and said, "Spazey, my boy!" He limped hurriedly over to embrace Spassel.

"I'm okay," Spassel said. "Sorry if I caused you any trouble."

"No, no, my dear boy. Don't you worry about me. I've been around long enough to know how to convince a Swartza I'm no threat."

Spassel turned to the group. "These are my friends who saved me. This is Nat," he pointed to Nathanial, "the one I was supposed to save. You know Mila already, and this is Gem and Aliya."

"Hello, everyone," Uncle Watt greeted them warmly. "Thank you all for being so brave and helping my nephew. It does my old heart good to see all this youth standing up so strongly together. I'd thought all hope was gone from this world until now."

"We're going to fix things, Uncle," Spassel said, and firmly shook his uncle's hands. "Sprites were opening their eyes to the possibilities of change just with the rumor of a human turned sprite, and if we can free Nat from this place they'll get to see that he's more than just a rumor, that real change is possible, that we don't have to be tied down to a blood trait and forced into a job we don't want just because we were born to it. We've been so close to progress, with factory-friendly operations opening up and Hyperion pulling in more students than ever. We can do this, Uncle Watt. We won't let her revert us to the dark ages."

Uncle Watt gave Spassel another big hug, then pulled away with renewed resolve in his eyes and said, "Then let's get you lot out of here and on your way to change the world."

Spassel laughed at the glee he saw in his uncle's eyes. But Nathanial wavered. He wasn't sure how he felt about being the poster boy of a revolution.

"I hate that this is the only way out," the uncle added, "but I know you can do it."

"What's the only way out?" Nathanial asked, looking around to see if he was the only one not getting it.

"The Dreg Chute," Uncle Watt clarified.

Nathanial looked to the others and read their expressions, which reflected his own. This was going to be messy.

Uncle Watt was helping Spassel up onto the counter, just in front of where the conveyer belt was dumping smelly chunks into the void, as he continued to give directions to the group. "When you come to the sorter, everyone hold tight to each other. Keep to the right of the chute with all the smaller foodstuffs. The big chunks go left into a chopper."

"A chopper!" Mila exclaimed as the others gasped.

"You should be able to avoid it easily. Just stay in the small pile," Uncle Watt said with certainty.

Nathanial saw the faltering in his friend's eyes and he knew he had to take action. His entire time at this school had been spent hunting for a way out, and this was the only one with no strings attached. He jumped up onto the counter and said, "Come on, guys, we can do this. Let's get out there and let everyone know what kind of crazy is going on in this school." He may not be comfortable being the poster boy of a revolution but he wasn't going to be quiet about the injustice and brainwashing he'd witnessed either.

Aliya climbed up to the edge of the chute; followed by Gem and Mila.

"Good luck," Uncle Watt said, looking to each

of them with a proud grin.

Nathanial gave Aliya an encouraging nod then turned to the Dreg Chute. A smell of rotted food wafted his way. He held his breath, sat down at the top of an aluminum slide, and pushed off onto the slippery slope.

He soon caught up to the food waste. His leg stabbed knee-deep into a tomato chunk and he shifted into a sideways spin. Flailing his arms to rotate his body forward again only plunged his elbows into a pile of worm guts and sent him sliding backward.

Nathanial soon heard chirping screams from the girls behind him. Each time there was a sudden drop Nathanial could hear their squeaks getting closer. They were catching up quickly and by the sounds of it they were all clumped together.

The food in front of Nathanial suddenly began piling up before him and his descent came to a crunching halt. His breath was then knocked out of him by his four friends colliding chaotically into his back with their feet, elbows, and heads in no particular order.

"Ugh." Spassel's strained breath sounded from somewhere under Gem's stomach. "We've hit the sorter. Everyone hold hands and get your backs to the right wall of the chute."

Nathanial took hold of the first hand he could find and started pulling it through the food toward the right. He couldn't see anything in the dark passage, but he could feel the pile of food bits dwindling underneath him. Then he felt something tug on his foot and he fell back. There was a conveyer belt under them sensing their weight. It started forcing them to the left.

"Ah!" Nathanial screamed. "It's trying to put us in the chopper!"

"We have to swim!" Aliya called out from behind Nathanial. "Swim on top of the mush. Kick away from the big food chunks."

"Uck," Nathanial said, trying to get over onto his belly.

The mush consisted largely of bug leftovers, the scrapings that weren't good to eat. It was the worst smell Nathanial had ever encountered in his life but the plan was working. The group was being pulled into the pool of gray muck while the large chunks fell to the left. But all too soon the feeling of triumph became panic. Nathanial was up to his chest in thick, putrid liquid that was starting to form a whirlpool. They were going to drown!

"Keep your head above the liquid as long as

possible," Spassel shouted as they began to spin toward the center of the large drain. "Only hold your breath right before you have to go under."

"Spassel, are you sure about this?" Nathanial asked. He himself was pretty sure they were about to die.

Spassel didn't answer.

A small tomato chunk loosened off Nathanial's leg. It had been sucked down the liquid tornado in front of him. Time to take that last breath. Filling his lungs until his rib cage stretched tight, Nathanial closed his eyes, and felt his body pulled into the vortex.

He was spinning like a dreidel; down, down, down. Disorientation, nausea, and impending death played a game of rock-paper-scissors in Nathanial's head.

The spinning stopped and Nathanial hit the sides of the tube several times before feeling himself go into free fall. There was just enough space around him that he could catch a breeze around his lips and exchange a new breath for the old before he splashed into a shallow muddy pond. He stumbled to get his footing and felt his friends plopping down all around him.

Nathanial wiped the gook out of his eyes and off

his face, spitting and spluttering. He was starting to help Aliya to her feet, and orient himself with their new exterior setting, when he froze. They were being watched. About a dozen dirty sprites with buckets and bags stood still around the edge of the pond. But just as suddenly as he'd spotted the figures they flew away to hide behind the piles of food waste.

"Everyone okay?" Nathanial asked the group, who were wringing bug bits out of various parts of clothing and hair. Nathanial looked around again. "Did anyone see that?"

"See what?" Aliya spat.

"There were sprites." Nathanial pointed vaguely around.

"They're scavengers that work the dregs. Often called dregs themselves," Mila said, making her way out of the mud. "You don't have to worry about them, they're harmless. Many of them were put to the dregs as punishment for misdemeanors, like ticking off Seizette. What we need to worry about is the Swartza guards who will be coming for us. Like I said, Seizette didn't want to give you two up. We need to move."

The group waded heavily out onto the bank and tried to get their bearings. They were behind the castle where large pipes dumped chunks of waste into several mountainous piles and ponds around them.

Mila took it upon herself to take the lead and said, "This way," as she darted between piles of vegetables.

"Do you actually know where you're going?" Nathanial asked, following close behind her.

"Yeah. Away from the castle," she responded shortly.

The group didn't object and, they stayed quiet as they walked close together. They passed beyond the piles of rot where dog-sized flies circled their treasure and into a forest until they could no longer hear the plopping of the dispensing pipes.

Soon they came to a river. Gem and Aliya immediately began to rinse off the putridity that clung to them.

"This is good," Mila said, looking around. "We should walk downstream for a while. It will make us harder to track."

"Isn't there a Niche or a bird or an air stream we could use?" Nathanial asked, not liking the slow pace of walking down a stream.

"Places like this make travel as strict as possible for security purposes. The few Niches in the area are Swartza-controlled and so is the wildlife. And no, no air stream. This is what we got." She gestured to the river.

But they didn't have the river either. Swartza guards surrounded them in moments. Like a swarm homing in they came from trees and sky. Dozens of them, from every side, holding batons and nets. There was nowhere to run.

RIVER RUN

"Stay close," Mila said, and they gathered together in the river. "It'll be harder for them to carry us in a single net. They'll want to separate us."

Nathanial wondered at Mila's knowledge of such tactics, but he still liked the advice and waited for further instructions. The guards had closed in to form a complete circle around them.

The Swartza in front addressed a sprite over his shoulder. "What are your orders, Captain? Shall we separate them?"

The captain stepped forward. It was Malik. "Hold the line," he said, looking seriously down at Nathanial. "I only want this one."

Nathanial stepped forward. He felt several hands grab hold of his shirt. "You only want me? You'd let the others go?"

"That's right," Captain Malik said softly.

"Why?" Nathanial didn't trust it of course. It didn't make sense. Seizette had enjoyed having Aliya, a victim of a broken oath; she couldn't just let her spy Spassel walk away; and Gem was supposed to be locked up as an example of what happened to those who helped humans. Why would he only take him? Maybe because Malik's vendetta had nothing to do with the others. Nathanial could see it in his hungry eyes. Seizette had said Malik wanted to prove to her that Nathanial didn't belong. And after all, Malik had been after him since the beginning.

"Does it matter why?" Malik said, lifting his eyebrows. "Come with me now and save your friends. This will be your only chance at that offer."

"Don't listen to him, Nat. He's just trying to break us up," Mila said, pulling Nathanial back toward her.

"I could break you up easy enough," Malik said with a chortle, and gestured to his troops. "It would hurt you more than it would hurt me. Oh right. It wouldn't hurt me at all."

A quiet fell. No one moved. Everyone waited.

"Fine." Malik backed away into his troops. "Take them all."

Dozens of hands reached in from all sides and pulled at Nathanial's limbs. He had hold of Aliya's and Mila's arms, and they had hold of Gem's and Spassel's, but the strength of the five young sprites was no match for that of the horde. They were soon ripped apart from one another.

Nathanial reached down and pulled his battle blade out from its sheath by his ankle but before he could raise it he was being wrapped up in a sticky net.

"Take me, just take me!" Nathanial was screaming but Malik scoffed.

"Too late," he said, and gestured a beckoning finger to the troops who held Nathanial. They carried his squirming form over to Malik, who bent down to whisper in his ear. "You're right," he said coldly. "I wouldn't have let your friends go. They all belong in the diamond, even Aliya for her traitorous bloodline; never trust the spawn of a traitor. But you are not even worth a place in the queen's diamond. You were born a factory, and a factory you should still be. I will finish what I started with you one day, and if you thought your room was a prison, just wait until you see the mental hospital I have in mind for you."

Nathanial held the cold stare. Anger boiled inside of him and he felt it course into the battle blade that he gripped tightly to his trapped side. Instinct took over and the knife exploded into a sword without command. The weblike net around him burst off into thousands of sticky strands and sent the guards that held him backward in surprise.

Nathanial brought up his sword in challenge to Malik.

A flash of shock sparked in Malik's eyes before he brought his own sword up with a look of delight. He held his hand up to stop the guards from retaking control of Nathanial and they backed off.

"You really are arrogant, aren't you," Malik said. "This should be fun."

Malik thrust his sword directly toward Nathanial's heart. Nathanial blocked but barely, the sword tip scraped his shoulder as it continued its forward momentum before Malik withdrew for his next attack.

There was no time for thought, only reactions. Nathanial was in full defense mode. Malik made several attacks in quick succession that Nathanial just managed to block. Malik was bigger, stronger, and more experienced. Nathanial was aware that he had lost the amulet that had given him his edge when sparring with Boss. Not only that but they were fighting in a river and the current that pressed against Nathanial's heels made every dodge all the more difficult.

Malik was about to come in for a punching thrust. He reared his sword far behind him but just then something flew over their heads and forced them both to duck.

Nathanial looked around and saw a full-on skirmish was afoot. The Swartza, who had wrestled Aliya, Spassel, Gem, and Mila to the riverbank, were being surrounded by flying sprites in plastic attire. It almost looked like trash bags had come for vengeance.

"What is this?" Malik grimaced.

Nathanial smiled. His friends were being rescued. "Looks like the tables are turning," he said to Malik, feeling a new surge of confidence within him. He lunged.

Now it was Malik that was on the defense. Nathanial used every trick he'd ever learned from Boss. With the dull side of his blade he would parry and then twist into the sharp side to thrust. The look on Malik's face was no longer smug. He had to concentrate intently to counter each attack. The new fighting dance was taking them farther downstream and the current hastened them in that direction until the sounds of the others were no longer audible.

Malik was clearly coming to the peak of his frustration when his leg lodged against a boulder in the river. He took the pressure as an opportunity and leaned toward Nathanial on his next lunge. Malik caught Nathanial's hilt against his own and used his large hands to hold it in place.

Malik pulled Nathanial in close to his face and said, "Enough. You are an abomination. You'll never be one of us. You should go back to the humans where you belong. You are weak. A scared little boy that will amount to nothing."

Nathanial thought about the truth in Malik's words. He'd often felt too small to fight the big problems in the sprite world and had considered just rescuing Aliya, going home, and leaving the politics of sprites well enough alone. But then he'd remembered how far he'd come with the help of some very special sprites. Mila and Spassel were two sprite friends close to his same age and they saw the corruption in their society and were willing to fight against it. Spassel even looked up to him as a symbol of the change that could come. Nathanial may have started as a weak, scared little boy, but the real thing about him, the thing that he felt defined him, was his ability to never give up, never stop wishing, and never stop fighting.

"You have no idea what I'm capable of," Nathanial said fiercely and he pushed away everything Malik stood for. He could feel the vibrations of this emotion funnel through his body and into the battle blade. A huge burst of invisible power expelled outward from the hilt, breaking the grasp, and forcing Malic away.

Malik and Nathanial flew apart from one another, Malik received the brunt of the blast, and he disappeared deep into the foliage beyond the river. Nathanial caught himself from falling backward and steadied himself in excited disbelief. He held up his battle blade and looked at it with new pride.

"Wow," he said astonished and then he heard a splash behind him.

Nathanial turned to see the remnants of a disturbance in the water but nothing was there. Then he heard the thunder. Slowly he looked to the sky and felt the ominous cold of a new wet breeze on the air. The grey rolling clouds sent a shiver of foreboding down Nathanial's spine.

Nathanial quickly stowed his blade back into its knife size sheath on his ankle and hurriedly began to wade his way toward the nearest shore. The water was rising quickly now, it was up to his knees and then another droplet splashed down next to him. Unfortunately his size was not large enough to tolerate even a sprinkle. It was as if a water bomb had landed next to him and he was swooshed up into the wake of the wave.

Suddenly Nathanial was swept downstream, only occasionally properly positioned to breathe gulps of air through his gaping mouth. The current was quickening. Where there had been small humps of white water before, now the river churned ceaselessly.

Nathanial focused his recall on a book he had read about white-water rafting. It had said that if you fall out of your boat, you should point your toes downstream and wait for your boat-mates to pick you up. Well, Nathanial was pointing his toes now but there was no boat around to help him, although he was able to keep his head above water in this new position; unfortunately that small triumph did not last. Ahead of him Nathanial saw a stick disappear into furling mist. He was approaching a waterfall.

There was nothing to be done for it. He watched as the cliff came upon him and he tumbled over it.

For a few heart-stopping moments the sensation of free fall overtook him. He was plummeting through the mist when a wrenching pain scraped up his back. A branch had caught hold of him and torn through his school uniform. Nathanial screamed in pain. He tried to reach for the branch. This movement only exacerbated the pain but allowed him a horrific view. Wings were jutting out from between Nathanial's shoulder blades; and were twisted into the branch.

Nathanial had never known such agony, and he

heard his own cries as if from a distance. His brain was trying to shut down. The hot poker in his back smothered all other sensations.

The branch snapped.

The drop was surely hundreds of feet but Nathanial had stopped seeing through his eyes; instead he saw only red flashing from within. He knew he was waiting for an impact and somehow thought it might be a mercy but just when he'd let the darkness consume him, he felt a sudden jolt around his waist. It took his breath away. Something or someone had caught him out of the air.

"I've got you," a voice said.

Nathanial tried to open his eyes, to see if it were true, to see if he was truly still alive, but he could not focus. The pain overwhelmed him and he passed out.

TROOP REGROUP

There were moments when Nathanial wasn't sure if he was dreaming or awake. He could hear voices echoing distantly in his mind and there was a subtle rocking. He felt like he was back in the carriage with the queen during the trials. He saw her beside him and she saw through and into him. Her sparkling red lips smiled at him and her teeth glistened with blood.

Then he opened his eyes. There were dim figures sitting around him. The rocking persisted. He really was in a carriage of some kind, lying on his stomach over a cushioned bench. The pain returned in the core of his spine and he groaned. A figure ran to him and waved something beneath his nose. The smell was sweet and comforting. The pain dulled and Nathanial slipped back into his dreams.

When he finally broke from the groggy confusion of half dreams, he was lying still and no longer in the carriage. He was on his stomach but in a bed surrounded by tan clay walls, with light pouring in through a small round window in the ceiling.

Nathanial tested his mobility. The pain in his back took away his breath but it was less than before. He could push through it, and he sat up. There was no one in the room. The wooden chair next to the bed had a rumpled blanket thrown over it, which told him someone had been keeping watch.

The shirt and pants that hung loosely off him were tan and somewhat fuzzy. A strange leather harness cupped around his chest and a new weight tugged at his back. There was also a twinge in his rib cage. He pulled up his shirt and saw a row of bandages there.

Nathanial looked to the wooden door across from him. Licking his lips, he slowly pushed off from the bed and stood momentarily bent over. Maybe he'd become an old man during his sleep. He definitely felt like one. Every time he slid one foot in front of the other there was an accompanying bone-popping noise. He didn't get more than a few feet before the door opened.

"What do you think you're doing?" Aliya cried out in shock and ran over to put her shoulder under his arm.

"Trying to walk," Nathanial said. "Didn't think

it'd be such a problem."

"Unfortunately that's just one of your problems," Boss said from the doorway.

Nathanial looked Boss up and down. For the first time since Nathanial had met him he was not in a suit. Blue was still the theme but now with buckles as well. His leatherlike, thigh-length jacket only partially concealed the sword strapped to his hip. His jeans had buckles that held knives just above his high strappy boots and the whole thing was tipped toward a steampunk style. Nathanial did not know what to make of it.

Boss took in Nathanial's stare and smiled. He walked the rest of the way into the room and asked, "Well, don't you have anything to say for yourself?"

Nathanial was taken aback. So much had happened to him, including gaining insight into Boss's past, and he had hoped to have a new respect for his mentor. But it was clear their relationship was still on unstable ground and he would have to defend his every action as usual. Boss was clearly seeking an apology for running off to save Aliya. Why couldn't Boss see that he had to do it?

Aliya caught the frustration growing in Nathanial's expression and said, "Boss saved your life. He saved all of us. He convinced the dregs to help him ambush the Swartza guards."

Boss was still smiling. Nathanial swallowed. He was going to say thank you but instead, "What did you mean by just one of my problems?" came out.

Boss sighed. "It's your wings," he said, rubbing his brow. "The roots were entangled during your fall, and they weren't ready to sprout, but they were close; given another week or so they would have come out softly and then hardened naturally over a couple days. Instead we've had to graft them with a variety of plant vascular tissues in order to shape and harden them. Your wings will be strong but the process makes them heavy, which means your body will have to be strong too."

"Seeing as I can barely walk, what does that mean?" Nathanial asked, bracing himself.

"It means you're going to have to practice some of that patience you so obviously love," Boss said sarcastically. Nathanial's lack of patience had been a reoccurring tension between them.

Boss walked around Nathanial. Aliya backed away to give them some space.

"What are you doing?" Nathanial asked. In his hunchback position he could not easily turn to see.

"Hold your breath," Boss said, and crossed his arms around Nathanial's chest.

Nathanial quickly did so and Boss yanked him

out of his stooped position. There was a moment of cracking pain and shock.

"Better?" Boss asked, letting go.

Nathanial stood straight up in place and then turned to look at Boss. "Yeah," he squeaked, feeling stiff as a board. He lifted his shirt, revealing the bandages, and asked, "And what's this all about?"

"Mila hypothesized that there was likely a tracking spike left in you from Malik's old arrow, the same one that had temporarily taken your memories. She was right. We removed it."

"Oh, finally," Nathanial said. "I'm so tired of that guy popping up. I was beginning to think he had some kind of mind tap on me."

Boss laughed. "That would be creepy, but mind taps are special to animal companions."

Nathanial furrowed his eyebrows. He thought he'd just made that up.

"Which reminds me," Boss continued, "there's someone who's been wanting to see you, but we'll get to that soon. Right now there's someone more important that you have to talk to."

Boss pulled a box out of his pocket. "You two should have a seat for this," he said, and took out a tiny gelatin ear cup. Nathanial had seen those things before, and he smiled. He took a seat on the bed next to Aliya and held his hand out for the offering. He put one of the squishy cups over his right ear and it shrank down.

"Wow," Aliya said, excited.

Nathanial took another cup out of the box and shrank the tip on his left ear.

"You too, Aliya." Boss held the box out to her. Aliya took it and the cups.

"I don't understand," Aliya said.

"You will," Boss said, and pulled a tablet out from his back pocket. Aliya put the cups over her ear tips.

Boss swiped the tablet and handed it to Nathanial. Nathanial had an idea of what was going on but he'd never used a tablet like this before and waited with excited anticipation.

Suzy's kind and expectant face filled the screen.

"Mom!" Nathanial cried out with joy. "Can you see me?"

"Yes, darling, I can see you! And it is so good to see you. I've missed you terribly!" Suzy said, her high brown ponytail swishing as she looked from him to Aliya. "Who's your friend?"

Nathanial couldn't believe this. This was amazing. He was getting to introduce his two favorite people to each other. "This is Aliya! She's my best friend. Aliya, this is my mom."

"Hello," Aliya said and waved to the screen.

"Your son is so brave, Mrs. Thatcher. He's helped me through more than I can say. You should be proud of him."

"Oh, call me Suzy, sweetheart, and thank you for saying that. It's good to know he has made a kind friend. I don't think he liked his friends very much at his last school and it just broke my heart. He was alone for so much of his life, as I'm sure he's told you."

"I had you, Mom," Nathanial said, his eyes glassy with emotion.

"Oh, baby, thank you. I just mean you deserve a good friend who isn't your mom."

They all laughed.

"Does this mean you're settling into the new school? Will you be wanting to stay?" Suzy asked, almost with trepidation.

Nathanial paused. He knew what she was asking. She wanted to know if he was choosing Hyperion over his old school back home. Boss had told her he'd be given the choice at the end of his first term. It would mean he wouldn't see his mom at all during the school year. He had been moving in that direction, but being faced with saying goodbye to his mom for so long was making it difficult to speak. He glanced up at Boss, who was nodding in encouragement, and mouthing, Say yes.

Nathanial pursed his lips and said, "Yeah, I think so, Mom. I'd like to stay through the school year if that's okay with you."

Suzy nodded, and her hard swallow told him she was holding back the waterworks. "That's good," she finally said. "I'm grateful that you had the opportunity to make this choice for yourself, Nathanial. You are taking control of your own life. I am beyond proud of you." She wiped the tear away before it could escape her eye.

"Thank you, Mom. I would be nothing without you. You saved my life."

At that she just let the tears flow. "Love you, baby," she said between sobs. "Now you go and enjoy yourselves, kids. This is a special time in your lives; don't forget to have some fun in between all those classes. It was lovely meeting you, Aliya. You two take care of each other, and I expect you to invite her to visit us this summer, Nathanial. We can all take a fun trip together."

"It was nice meeting you too, Suzy. I look forward to meeting you in person," Aliya said, having a hard time keeping control of her own emotions.

"Bye, Mom. I'll call again, soon this time, promise. I love you," Nathanial said.

"Love you." Suzy waved.

Nathanial and Aliya waved back. The screen

went black. Nathanial put the tablet down and gave Boss a grateful look. "Thank you," he said, and he meant for everything.

Boss nodded with a knowing smile and took back the tablet. Aliya put her ear cups back into the little box and handed it to Nathanial, who did the same. He held the box out to Boss.

"No, you keep them," he said, and shook the tablet before setting it down on Nathanial's bedside table. "You'll need them for when you call your mom again."

Nathanial rubbed his chest where his amulet used to be. Mila had shown him how to shrink his ears once, without the ear cups, but he wasn't sure he could do it without his tap-aid necklace. He set the little box down by the tablet.

"If you're feeling up to it we have others who would like to say hello," Boss said.

The exhilaration from speaking to his mom was still running through Nathanial's veins, and he said, "Yeah, I'm good."

Boss led Nathanial and Aliya up a set of spiraling clay steps that glowed with orange and red iridescence. He pushed up a trapdoor in the ceiling and they came out on a hilltop that overlooked a small dirt training yard, with grassy mound huts along its edges. They looked like something Bilbo

Baggins might live in.

"Whoa, what is this place?" Nathanial asked.

"This is one of many sanctuaries that have cropped up over the last few months," Boss said as they watched sprites spar with wooden sticks while others played tricks that made grass grow suddenly and reach out to capture their sparring partners. "Sprites who made pro-factory products, or granted wishes that disrupted factory production, or tried to change their colors have all been disappearing and getting replaced by Swartza loyalists. Even Hyperion is under lobby to be shut down. Seems we turned a blind eye to all those conspiracy theories for too long."

"What conspiracy theories?" Nathanial asked seriously.

"That Seizette only signed the Crossing Treaty and stepped down from power because she had a plan to return. We've just found a loophole in the treaty that must have been written in at the last minute, as it wasn't in any of the drafts before. It gave Seizette ultimate authority on key positions during elections that have been taking place over the decades. A couple of months ago she put my old boss in charge of all Grit the Gook companies, giving him a monopoly and allowing him to get rid of all factory-friendly products. Human hospitals are getting very crowded these days."

"So there is a rebellion coming," Nathanial said, watching the sprites practice fighting.

Boss stiffened and looked down at Nathanial. "Where did you hear that?"

"Seizette. She's been training her troops at that school for who knows how long. She's got them all hyped up, saying the rebels could attack any day. She has them brainwashed to think she's in the right. That to be against her is to be against freedom."

"There are no rebels," Boss said flatly.

"Then what do you call that?" He gestured before them.

"They're learning to defend themselves and their families, that's all."

"But, but don't they know she's going to take over?"

"Sprites live a long time. We have long memories. No one wants another rebellion. Many of us were there for the last one."

"But you're going to stand up to her at least, right, like you did before? You could lead these people."

Boss narrowed his eyes at Nathanial, who gulped. Boss surely wanted to keep his secret under wraps, but Nathanial couldn't help it. He had seen what

Boss was capable of. He was a hero! Seizette had cursed him, crushed his spirit, and stripped him of his title, but surely Boss had worked through that curse by now. Nathanial had seen him in action, fighting a beetle back when Boss was escorting him to his wish hearing, and defending him from Malik more than a couple of times! Maybe all he needed was his title back. What would happen if Nathanial said Boss's real name?

"If there is any fight to come, it will have to be a political one, and I am no politician," Boss finally answered and looked away.

"You know she's already won that fight." Nathanial sighed.

Aliya had kept very quiet during the conversation but here she took a breath and joined in. "I have seen what conflict of ideals does to a people. My mother died in service to ours, and my sister has surely faced it in my absence. My father always told us when we were growing up that by the time we were old enough to serve, the fighting would be over. But it is never over. I guess I've always feared my fate would come to this. I just had the wrong battlefield in mind."

Boss looked solemnly down at Aliya. "We aren't going to allow our youth to pick up the fight where we left off," he said, shaking his head. "We still have a chance. Seizette has been brought down before. She's not yet in a position to do much more than spread rumors of a rebellion. We can still take control of the situation."

Timid hope gleamed in Aliya's eyes.

Nathanial looked over to her. He shared her fearful hope. Seizette seemed powerful but maybe Boss was right. If the civilian population of sprites could just see the truth of what was happening, surely they'd put a stop to it. Even the Roman emperors had feared the mob, and the mob was exactly what had forced Seizette to step down the first time.

"I hope you're right," Nathanial said.

Boss sighed and brushed his fingers through his thick dark hair. "Well, I don't want you two worrying about it anymore. You're safe here, so let's drop the subject for now. I brought you up here to see someone, after all."

Boss cupped his hands around his mouth and made a noise that sounded exactly like a raven's caw. Moments later, a black shadow passed over them and dropped down with the beating of massive silken wings.

"Sidian!" Nathanial exclaimed in excitement. "But you work for the Swartza. I was sure I'd never see you again."

The raven clicked his beak for several seconds, letting out intermittent caws. Aliya looked dumbfounded as she watched Nathanial laugh and nod his head.

"Yeah, I know she's crazy," Nathanial said, patting Sidian's beak. He caught Aliya's expression and added, "He said he knew I was trying to reach him in Swartza High. He tried contacting me several times but Seizette had electrified the windows! That's the noise we heard, Aliya. Can you believe it? Sidian was trying to help us the whole time!"

Boss smirked, saying, "Well, you've made him a rebel at least. He's asked me if he can be your companion. I told him to stick around during your training and we'll see."

"Really!" Nathanial excitedly exclaimed. "That would be so cool."

The grassy door opened behind them and a welcoming troop flowed out. Gem and Bunny appeared first, chattering something about the insanity of angering the wish sprites; Mila and Spassel followed after. The door was shutting when it hit Phlegm on the head as he came grumbling out.

"Hey Nate-a-roony!" Bunny ran up quickly and gave Nathanial a tight but considerate-of-his wing-bandages kind of hug. "You did it! You found Gem," she said, bouncing with joy.

"I think she kind of found me." Nathanial smiled.

"We all found each other," Gem said sweetly.

"I can't believe you have wings," Spassel said to Nathanial.

"I know," Nathanial agreed.

"They're going to take some upkeep," Spassel said knowingly. "But I can help you out with that."

"Oh, what do you know about wings?" Mila teased Spassel.

"I had an uncle who grew some wings later in life," Spassel explained.

"Another uncle." Mila rolled her eyes.

Everyone laughed.

It was weird seeing all his friends grouped together like that. Nathanial hadn't realized the horde he had collected. It was a good feeling. Even if Phlegm still liked to make remarks that insinuated Nathanial had ruined his life, he couldn't completely hide his relief at seeing Nathanial okay.

"So you're all going to be staying here?" Nathanial asked the group at large.

"Well, yeah," Mila said, putting a hand on her hip. "It's clear we're all a little too pro-moral to be accepted into the ever-growing unethical society that's infested our world today. This is as good a place to regroup as any, I'd say."

"I don't know how pro-mor-al I am," Phlegm said in his Brooklyn accent, "but I've never been one to back down from my responsibilities, and thanks to this one's sister"—he pointed to Bunny—"you're still one of them, kid."

"Well, I'm glad to have you," Nathanial said politely, deciding to keep things civil with Phlegm. Phlegm's expression softened.

Everyone started to pair off as they looked down at the training refugees and spoke of their next move. Aliya hooked her arm around Nathanial's.

"I want to train with you," she said intrepidly. "I know Boss doesn't think there is a fight coming, and I hope he's right, but my people didn't want a fight either. The thing is when you back the most docile creature in the world into a corner, you can still expect a bite."

Nathanial sighed. "And it's only a matter of time before Seizette puts us all in a corner."

Aliya nodded.

Standing on that hilltop with the knowledge that a mad queen was on the rise, Nathanial should have been feeling nothing but dread. But he had Aliya on his arm, Sidian standing over his shoulder, and all his friends lined up beside him.

The ache in his back only meant he was going to have to grow strong, and thanks to everyone around him he was no longer the sickly boy who only saw the world through books and a computer screen. Now he could do anything he put his mind to, and he owed it to his companions to take action.

Nathanial felt Aliya pull in closer as the sun began to set and the air turned chilly. Yes, Seizette had to be stopped for many reasons, but the one holding him tight in that moment would have been enough.

Not Quite The End

Look for the conclusion to Nathanial Thatcher's adventure in:

The Fourth Rebellion